Praise for William Meikle

"One of the premier storytellers of our time."
—Famous Monsters of Filmland

"Big beastie horror seems to be all the rage right now. Unfortunately, very few authors seem to know how to do it right. They need to take lessons from Meikle. He's at the top of his class."
—Into the Macabre

"*The Dunfield Terror* is... another masterpiece from Mr Meikle – one that should grace the bookshelf of any fan of those genres, or simply those who appreciate fine writing."
—The Sci-Fi and Fantasy Reviewer

"*Fungoid* is... a fast paced ecohorror thriller that delivers on all fronts. The large cast of characters combined with Meikle's tight plotting and a keen eye for dialogue bring a real cinematic feel to the narrative. By focusing more on the fast based plot rather than getting bogged down by over characterisation Meikle has created a real page-turner."
—Ginger Nuts of Horror

A MURMURATION OF OPAS

A MURMURATION OF OPAS

WILLIAM MEIKLE

DARK MOONS

Text © 2023 by William Meikle

Cover art and interior and cover design © 2023 by Cyrus Wraith Walker

Editor and Publisher, Joe Morey

ISBN: 978-1-957121-50-5

DARK MOONS

Weird House Press
Central Point, OR 97502
www.weirdhousepress.com

For Ray Bradbury, John Carpenter, Ray Harryhausen and Ridley Scott, all of whom went into the Opa soup.

CHAPTER 1

When the submersible descended out of the tube on the twenty third of October, in the year twenty one eighty, Jodge Chong became the first human to travel under the ice on Europa. He was more aware of history at that moment than he'd been in all the years it had taken him to get to this point.

"That's one small drop for a man, another giant leap for mankind," he said into the com, and heard the others laugh in his ear. It did a lot to relieve the tension that had been building since he'd entered the tube half an hour earlier and ten miles higher.

Conjecture about Europa and the possibility of life there had been going on for two centuries. A variety of unmanned spacecraft had mapped and photographed and surveyed over the years, and several robots had been sent down to the surface to collect and retrieve samples but although they had found complex hydrocarbon molecules there had never been any proof of life. They needed a manned mission, and they needed to drill, for if there was life on the moon, it was going to be in the ocean, locked away under miles of ice where it might have been floating there for millennia.

Jodge was involved from the start, as diving consultant at first while the Earthside administrators and scientists tried to come up with a plan, then more directly after the Io mission was done and he could be spared. He had just made it home to Mars from that one by a month when they recruited him for Europa. He hooked up with the outgoing mission in the asteroid belt, and spent some time getting to know the others in the long dark stretch between there and Jupiter while Anna built her team and Jodge built his submersible.

Now here they were.

Making history.

It hadn't been an easy mission, having been a political and logistical nightmare from the start, fraught with difficulty, and turned out to be the longest, most expensive, most dangerous scientific mission of all time. Lives had been lost, companies had prospered, folded and prospered again, and all manner of scientific breakthroughs had, of necessity, been made on the hoof. All to bring Jodge to this point, hanging at the bottom of a drill hole ten miles down in a small submersible as it passed beneath the ice and reached the Europa Ocean proper.

He was thinking about the long line of those who had gone before: Magellan, Amundsen, Armstrong and Tsung and more, all the way back to the first human to look up, wonder what was beyond the horizon, and decide to go and have a look. He felt he should say something more, but it was Armstrong's words that continued to echo in his head.

Besides, this mission was already deemed a success before he'd even gotten into the sub; samples taken by a bot they'd sent down the tube first had proven that life was not merely an earthbound phenomenon. After all the disappointments of finding nothing but dust on Mars and only saturated salt water on Ganymede and Io, here they had finally found proof that humankind was not alone in the solar system, never mind the Universe.

The fact that it was, in Jodge's mind, a slightly disappointing proof was neither here nor there; although they'd only found a single species of unicellular life, they'd found an abundance of it in the samples taken so far by the bots. Davide and N'tini, being biologists, had given it a double-barrelled Latin name, but everybody else just called them Opas.

Now Jodge was here to see if they could find something else, maybe something a bit more complex. The Opas were making him work for it. They swarmed around the submersible, as ephemeral as smoke rising from a fire, swirling in an intricate dance that threw up patterns and curves in dizzying washes of bioluminescence. Davide and N'tini had a word for that too; murmuration. It was a word generally applied to massive flocks of small birds back on earth. Jodge, who had never been Earthside, only had holovid clips to compare with. The ones on Earth didn't match up. The swirls around the submersible pulsed and glowed in an ever-changing blue-green aurora that, after some initial disorientation, he found almost calming.

It was all very pretty, but Jodge was here to go deeper, to see if there might be more to the ecosystem than just one dominant species. He was going to be sorely disappointed if all there was to see was a lot of Opas, a pretty dance, and nothing else. He also wasn't about to get too excited until he had proof; back on Io he'd gotten everybody's pulses racing when he'd reported seeing something moving purposefully in the water; it had turned out to be a lump of ice caught in a current, and he was still trying to live that one down.

"Are you okay?" a voice spoke in his headset.

"In the pipe, five by five," Jodge replied, knowing that he'd be the only one on the mission to get the antique reference,

"So that's a yes, then?" Anna Kaminski asked.

As Mission Commander Anna was his sole contact with the surface for the duration of the dive. Everybody else up there would be gathered round the holovids viewing the feeds he was sending back from the various cameras and sensors, hoping for a glimpse of something wondrous.

But only Anna can understand how it feels.

Like him, she'd been a diver, and they'd worked together on Io during the explorations there more than a decade previously. Where Jodge had never grown out of his love for the quiet solitude to be found on a solo deep dive, Anna had moved on, through various administrative levels, until now she outranked him by quite some way, her being commander of the mission, him being general dogsbody when he wasn't in charge of the sub.

He wouldn't have it any other way.

"Are you ready to take her down?" she asked.

There were a multitude of questions wrapped inside that simple one, and an equal multitude of answers came to mind, but he settled for the simple one.

"Ready as I'll ever be. Dropping her by five."

The sub responded to his neural link and descended five meters. The Opas moved with him, as if including him in some intricate dance to which only they knew the steps. Their color shifted towards a more yellow edge of the spectrum before settling back to the now familiar blue-green.

"Is this all getting recorded?" he asked.

The A.I. spoke in his ear.

"Ten channels, fore and aft, above and below. I'm getting everything."

They'd long decided not to give the A.I. a name; mainly because it was just too close to being human and at least half the mission team were uncomfortable with anthropomorphizing it any further than calling it 'her'. Jodge had long been one of the uncomfortable ones. Mars hadn't progressed as quickly technology wise as Earthside; he'd grown up with robots, sure, but not with a tech that could second-guess him at every turn, and was faster at the basics of the day-to-day stuff required to run a complex research station. It did its job well enough though, and Jodge was grateful it was keeping an eye on him down here in the dark.

Doesn't mean I need to have a conversation with it.

As the sub descended through them the Opa appeared to swirl and coalesce into a slightly more coherent form, and not for the first time Jodge wondered if there was more to them than just a swirling mass of cells. At times he thought there might even be some attempt at communication going on in the patterns and swirls, but as yet the A.I hadn't been able to make any correlations.

Jodge concentrated on taking the sub deeper. There might be all sorts of wonders out there beyond the blue-green aurora.

But I'll never see it if I never get clear of the Opas.

He descended another five meters, then five more.

"Steady," Anna said in his ear. "Easy does it."

The sub creaked and groaned. The pressure was enormous down here, but he knew the sub's limits better than anyone; he'd designed it himself and, along with the team's technicians, Rohit and Mark, had spent countless hours building, refining, testing and refining again during the long flight from the asteroid belt to here.

"She can take it," he replied confidently.

"I'm not sure I can."

"We're getting somewhere. The Opas are thinning out. Just a bit deeper."

He descended five more meters. The Opas finally gave up on him and hung in a swirling swarm above the sub. He couldn't see his descent hole through them, but the sub's beacon to the dome high above would steer him home even if he went blind.

He ordered the headlights to full power. The water was clear around him and the beams gave him a view a hundred meters ahead. It looked like open water, no sign of life save for the ceiling of swirling Opas overhead. His sensors told him the water was getting warmer as he descended; now at two degrees Celcius where it had been just a fraction above freezing in the drill tube.

"Temperature consistent with the theory," he said. "That's a point to the folks at NASA back in the Twentieth Century."

"Almost cozy compared to the surface temperature," Davide said in his ear.

"I wouldn't go that far, but I might stay here a while."

"Let's keep the chatter down, boys," Anna said. "We're on the clock here. You've got half an hour then it's time to come home."

Time to explore.

He started the sub forward, no more than a slow walking pace. His sensors recorded every small variation in pressure, temperature, salinity and oxygen content of the water around him, streaming the data back up top to the A.I. for processing. All he had to worry about was steering the sub and keeping his eyes open. He swept a wide area under his drop point in slowly increasing circles until he was at a widest point some four hundred meters to the north. There had been nothing but open water, then his lights caught a darker shadow ahead of him. His sonar pinged at the same moment, confirming that there was definitely something there. He couldn't make out what it was, but it didn't look like an Opa swarm; it looked like something more solid.

What if it's just ice again?

He kept his voice noncommittal.

"I may have something here," he said. "Moving in for a closer look."

"Remember, slow and steady," Anna said.

He had to remind himself of her remark as he closed in on the object for the more he saw of it, the more he wanted to see. The thing was bioluminescent, although not to the same degree as the Opas above; a bluish haze hung uniformly six inches around an amorphous body that was almost globular. A visual estimate had it at some three meters in diameter and it didn't appear to have any means of propulsion, traveling at the mercy of whatever currents were in the area.

At first glance it looked like a tangled mass of free-floating kelp, but as Jorge got closer he saw long trailing tendrils hanging from beneath it. They were so long that they trailed away into the dark depths beyond the range of his lights, and they too glowed faintly with the same blueish luminescence.

As he approached his lights washed over the dangling tendrils. The aurora changed to an almost golden color and the tendrils wafted and grasped, as if seeking the light.

"Are you seeing this?" he asked.

Anna came back immediately.

"There's some pretty excited people up here. It looks like some kind of jellyfish analogue. Or maybe a filter feeder do you think?"

"I'll need to get closer to find out. I'll get a sample of tissue if I can."

She didn't say it, but he heard it anyway... *be careful.*

He took the sub in slowly. The thing was drifting away from him. He circled and came up behind it and slightly above to ensure he kept away from the hanging tendrils. As he got closer and his lights caught it, the creature's surface trembled, almost like a shiver running through it. He backed away and approached again, with the same result.

"It must have sensory organs," Anna said. "It's light sensitive. It knows you're there."

"So now we're even," Jodge said. He extended the sampling arm. The creature shivered again, and recoiled when the arm touched it. Its aurora flared, almost as bright as the sub's headlights. Before he could back away the mass of tendrils whipped up in the water and wrapped tightly around the sub, blocking Jodge's view. They immediately started to squeeze, as if trying to crack the sub like an egg.

Jodge attempted to dislodge the thing. He still had propulsion, that was something, but the thing came with him as he tossed the sub first one way then the other. It gripped the vessel tighter. Jodge pushed the speed to maximum, and headed upwards; maybe the Opa swarm would distract it.

Red alert, Red alert. Hull breach imminent.

The warning echoed around the small cabin of the submersible.

"Get out of there," Anna shouted in his ear.

"What do you think I'm trying to do?"

He headed upwards at high speed, following the beacon, flying blindly due to the writhing, squirming mass of tendrils that fought against him all the way. He looked down at the monitor; he was approaching the Opa layer fast, but the tendrils still refused to loosen their grip. The Opa cloud went into a frenzied, swirling dance, sending out rapid pulses of multi-coloured lights in a dazzling aurora. The tendrils responded by gripping the sub even tighter.

He could feel the pressure build now, and had to equalize by holding his nose and blowing into his ears. It helped, but not much.

The sub, and the beast holding on to it, entered the Opa cloud, and the light show got even brighter, a swirling rainbow dance of color. Jodge piloted the sub on instinct alone, trying to follow the beacon. He made for the drop zone and the tube up through the ice.

"I'm coming up," he said. "And I won't be taking my time."

The trip back up the tube seemed to take forever. The red alert message kept blaring, Anna kept asking if he was okay, the tendrils didn't loosen their grip…but the hull held, and they kept rising, although it was slow going.

The A.I. came through at about the halfway point.

"I've been analyzing the data collected so far. The creature is clearly light sensitive."

"So where does that get us?" Jodge asked.

"Well, I've been wondering what might happen if there was no light."

"Why didn't I think of that?" Jodge said.

"I guess that's why they pay me the big bucks," the A.I. replied.

Jodge switched off all of his lights, both headlights and cabin; he was flying blind anyway so it wasn't a problem. He got a reaction almost immediately. One by one the tendrils loosened their grip and fell away from the hull. He saw the bioluminescent aura of the creature drift away, heading back down the tube while the sub took Jodge upwards.

There was a reception committee waiting for him on his return to the dome. Anna was the first to reach him once he'd gotten out of the sub. He didn't have time to get out of his suit. She punched him, hard, on the shoulder.

"You nearly got yourself killed."

"Nearly," Jorge admitted, and held her at arm's length. "But look, I'm still here. And I got a sample."

"You got more than that," a voice said at his back. Anna's head biologist Davide Thibaut was beside the sub, scraping organic material off the hull.

"This merde is all over it. It'll need to be decontaminated."

"Sample first, decontaminate later," Anna said. She stepped inside Jorge's arms and embraced him tightly.

"It was supposed to be slow and steady," she said.

"Tell the creature that next time; it was on me before I could react."

"Yes, we saw. They're going to name it after you."

"Whatever it is."

"Hopefully your samples will tell us. Once you're decent, meet us in the lab. We've got work to do."

Jodge showered and changed in the decon unit in the Drill Dome…that's what everyone called it. Its official designation was Europa Biodome Three, EB3 for short. There were currently three domes on site; the one containing the drill hole, one for the team's living quarters, designated EB1 and containing bedrooms, washrooms, medical room and mess room, and a third, EB2 containing the labs and scientific equipment. Since their arrival their main job had been installing and operating the drill, which was more in the way of a large heating unit than anything else. And they hadn't been actually drilling as such, merely melting and widening an existing, long dormant vent that ran all the way from the sea below to the surface, ten miles above. They'd got that job finished earlier than planned, and begun sampling operations. Today had been Jodge's first manned dive on site here. It hadn't exactly gone to plan. He was mulling how he'd approach the inevitable inquest conversation as he showered, and then once dressed, made his way quickly to EB2.

The domes were connected by a series of short corridors. EB1 also had a connecting corridor to the landing craft airlock, their lifeline between the surface and their mothership in a geosynchronous orbit overhead. They had life support capability for a team of thirty, although currently there were only six of them on site, four more in the mother ship, and a larger team still incoming in transit from Earth who were due in two weeks time.

He paused in the corridor between the domes to take in the view; he stopped almost every time he walked this way. He'd never been able to help himself.

It's just too damn beautiful.

It was daylight, or what passed for it here, but the sun wasn't the dominant thing in the sky; that was Jupiter, the huge bulk of the gas giant looming just above the far horizon. Below that lay Europa itself, a vast plain of ever-shifting ice and vents. The domes were built on the most stable area of ice they could find on the planet, but even then there were emergency evacuations systems drilled into everybody for possibly the inevitable, time when even that stable ice would shift. The ice itself, although flattened by lasers for an area around the domes and landing area, was a field of jagged pinnacles, like a graveyard of long dead, now skeletal, sea creatures, their bones reaching for the stars. A vent flared in the far distance, sending a rainbow shimmering across the horizon. He'd often wished he could just open a door and take a walk out on it, but he wasn't authorized for surface recon, and without one of the bulky suits required, he'd be a popsicle in seconds.

"Jodge?" Anna asked in his earpiece, "Are you on your way or are you at the window woolgathering again? There's something you need to see."

He reluctantly pulled himself away from the window and made for the lab.

The team was all present. Normally they worked in pairs and rotated shifts; Mark and Rohit should be in bed, but the two instrument techs were there alongside Anna, Davide and N'tini, all of them too excited to do anything but crowd around the holo. Jodge was surprised to see what they were looking at.

"Why are you looking at the Opas? Where's my sample?"

"This is your sample," Davide said. "And this is the one I scraped off your hull."

The holo flickered...and showed only more Opas.

"I don't understand," Jodge said.

"We've been talking about it," Davide replied. "We think the large one you tangled with was some sort of colony, a bunch, a big bunch, of Opas working in tandem with each other. Back on Earth some slime molds collaborate in this way in dynamic collectives. I think this is similar. But as soon as we broke a bit off the main organism, it reverted to its single cell state."

"But it looked like a jellyfish."

"And I suspect if we go deeper we'll find other Earth-type analogues; the Opas obviously collaborate and adapt to fit their environment. We've now seen the equivalents of the phytoplankton layer and one of the near surface feeders. I wouldn't be too surprised if we don't find something that looks almost like a fish…or even a whale if we go deeper."

"What do you mean, if…I've got another drop to do tomorrow."

"We've been talking about that too," Anna said. "Given what happened today, I'm considering canceling manned dives."

"We've been over that. We weren't getting enough info from the robots. You need my eyes down there, my experience."

"We also need you alive."

"It was my mistake," Jodge said. "When I saw it react the first time I should have backed off completely. It won't happen again."

Anna didn't argue with him.

But she didn't say no either.

They all watched the Opas float in their suspension for a while, but Jodge found them rather uninteresting, in their single cell form at least. They looked like another Earth organism that Jorge had studied in school back on Mars, a Paramecium, although the Opas had thicker cell walls, no obvious nuclei, and stronger, thicker cilia to propel them through the water. These ones in the sample were just hanging in suspension and none of them had moved for several minutes.

Finally even Davide, the most enthusiastic among them, decided he'd seen enough.

"Let's get these samples secured," he said. "And we'll hope for better luck next time."

Anna threw Jodge a look.

"I'm going to have to persuade you, aren't I," Jodge said.

Her smile didn't quite reach her eyes.

"Coffee first, persuasion later."

The team had split naturally into couples on the long flight out from Beta station in the asteroid belt; it hadn't been planned, or at least, if it was, Jodge hadn't known anything about it, only that he was happy with the outcome despite their differences.

Jodge was Mars born and bred, with the inherent physiological attributes that came with it; he was nearly seven feet tall, and rangy, with long fingers, a head that was thinner than it was long. narrow lips and eyes that looked slightly too large for his face. Anna was earthborn, of northern European heritage, and had inherited an almost stocky frame, muscular at shoulder and thigh. Her head barely came up to his chest.

They were as dissimilar in attitude as they were in appearance; Anna was ambitious, keen to move up the command chain, and saw herself heading for a job in the higher reaches of the Space Administration at some point. As for Jodge, all he wanted to do was dive.

Somehow it all worked. Anna was a natural leader, and he was, for the most part, happy to follow. But she could be stubborn when she put her foot down, and he'd seen that look she'd given him.

"Come on, Anna," he said as they stood by the coffee machine. "I got the sample."

"You nearly got dead, that's what you got," she said. "You're not going down again."

"I can be very persuasive."

"Don't try that Mars boy charm on me."

Jodge smiled.

"How about Europa boy charm?"

CHAPTER 2

Davide was supposed to be storing the latest samples, but he couldn't take his eyes off the holovid recording, not of the Opa as such, but of the creature they had come together to create. Before Jodge's dive Davide had almost convinced himself there was nothing more to be found, that the Opas were enough in and of themselves and anything more was just wishful thinking. To have uncovered a complex organism on their first manned dive suggested that he'd been far too conservative in his hopes.

This was Davide's first time out beyond Mars; after getting his degree Earthside he'd spent the bulk of his twenty year career on Mars Station, sifting through dirt hoping against hope that there would be a speck of life in it. To go from that to the Opas was like walking into a big, all-you-can-eat-buffet and he was currently struggling as to which aspect of the Opas he should be concentrating on first. This new creature had made his mind up for him.

Jodge's cameras had captured the creature in its entirety. Davide calculated the central mass to be almost three meters in diameter, and the trailing tendrils had to be fifty meters long, at least. There were tens, probably hundreds of millions of OPA cells in this thing, all cooperating in a way he could not yet fathom.

It was a biologist's wet dream, and his worst nightmare all rolled into one. He'd already been spending most of his waking moments trying to figure out how the photic layer Opas murmuration worked. He knew that, back on Earth, murmurations formed when one bird, starlings in the flock being the best example, copied the behavior of its seven neighbors, and then those nearby birds copied each of their seven neighbors, and so on until the entire group moved as one. He'd asked the A.I. to confirm that was the same case with the Opas, but the data was proving to be inconclusive at best, downright infuriating at worst. And now here they were making structural colonies.

"How are they doing it? It has to be chemical…hormonal," he muttered.

"I agree," N'tini said at his side. "I know we're supposed to be off shift, but this has me intrigued. Can we work on it?"

N'tini was a veteran off-worlder, having been a marine biologist on both the Io and Ganymede missions. California by birth, quiet and thoughtful by nature, she was known for her methodical approach to the work. Davide had also come to find she was playful and humorous in her free time, at least with him, and he had come to depend on her, not just to get the job done, but to keep him from falling into periodic bouts of depression when he considered the vast empty spaces they currently inhabited.

Officially speaking, Davide was the boss of the team by dint of superiority, but she was ice to his fire, and they made a good working partnership. He'd come to trust her judgment over the course of the mission, and he knew she'd be like a dog after a bone until she got to the bottom of the matter.

"I think we can afford a couple of hours on it," he said. "If neither us or the A.I. hasn't come up with something by then, we'll call it a day."

"Eighty-five hours," the A.I. said.

"What?"

"That's what I call a day, at least here."

Like Jorges, Davide was unsure of the A.I.. Sometimes it was almost as if it was telling a joke that only it thought funny, as with the previous quip, but everything was delivered in a flattish tone that wasn't quite monotone but didn't hold much in the way of nuance. He tried to avoid using it for his own work. N'tini, on the other hand, was all in for it, and an enthusiastic proponent of letting it do the donkey work.

"Let's get some of these new Opas into some growth medium," he said to the A.I.. "We can monitor all the chemical reactions, see if there's anything obvious going on."

The A.I. had the bots transfer a dozen Opa cells into a flask and Davide hooked it up to the Refractive Spectrometer so they could follow the chemistry in real time. They set the flask temperature to the same as the water in the ocean below and moved to the holo display. N'tini's warm hand slid into his and clutched tight.

"We're making history, right at this moment. We're the first to study this," she said.

"And it's being recorded for posterity. I'll try to mind my manners," Davide replied. He got a squeeze of the hand in reply, then they both concentrated on watching the Opas.

To begin with nothing of note happened; the Opas floated serenely, separately, in the medium, their thick cilia barely moving. There was no sign of any chemical interaction between them. They looked like what they were, individual cells, minding their own business.

"Maybe they need some kind of stimuli before they'll cooperate," N'tini said. "What can we try?"

"The obvious one first," Davide replied, and ordered the system to add more sugars to the growth medium. They waited ten minutes, but there was still no reaction from the Opas.

"Let's try temperature," N'tini suggested.

They spent almost half an hour both raising and lowering the temperature in the flask, and still got no movement from the cells. Adjusting the pressure in the flask likewise had no effect.

"There must be something," N'tini said.

Just at that moment the lights in the dome flickered, a common enough occurrence as the connection between the lighting system and the Fission Generator they had installed was proving to be flaky. Mark and Rohit had promised to have it sorted out soon, but it was a minor matter at best and they hadn't gotten around to it yet. It did, however, give Davide an idea.

"Remember how the colony responded when Jodge got the sub too close to it? He had his headlight on full at the time. Maybe it's the light."

He dimmed the lights in the lab area then had the system focus a bright beam on the glass flask. The result was immediate. All of the twelve Opas moved towards the light source, coming closer together as they did so. When Davide switched off the light they began to drift apart again.

"Now we're getting somewhere."

They experimented with different intensities of light, longer and shorter durations of having it switched on, but their breakthrough came when they rapidly switched the light on and off at high intensity. The Opa responded by clumping together and fluorescing in time with the pulse of the light. N'tina left Davide's side and began feeding the A.I. its instructions. Soon they had a dancing array of multicolored lights being shone on the flask. The Opa responded in kind, swirling around each other in an ever more rapid dance, always keeping time with the pulse of the lights.

"It's definitely a photic response," David said. "But there's still no chemical activity. How do they coordinate it?"

It took another hour or so to get an answer.

"I think I've got it," N'tini said. "They appear to have an internal clock that allows them to respond not just to an external light stimulus, but to the light being generated by the other Opa."

"There's no nucleus, nor any sign of an organelle that might provide such functionality," Davide protested.

"Nevertheless, the data is conclusive. Each Opa is capable of both responding to light and emitting light in complex sequences."

"And that's how they coordinate? How would that work?"

"Possibly it goes back to your murmuration theory; they could all be monitoring their neighbors simultaneously."

"If they are, it's a pattern I can't see. Not yet."

Davide set the A.I. to trying to make sense of the mathematics of it.

N'tini took his hand again as they watched the Opa dance while the A.I. tried to learn the moves. After five minutes it was clear a quick outcome wasn't going to be forthcoming.

"This could take some time," he said. "Shall we have coffee?"

≡

They walked through the corridor between the lab and the living quarters, and stopped by the viewing window. Dusk was falling on Europa, the icy towers throwing stark shadows across the ground, the sun going down, a large star on the horizon, the bulk of Jupiter dominating the whole sky. Davide still couldn't quite get used to the fact that Jupiter was always there, no matter what time of the Europa day you looked out of the window. Like Earth's moon, Europa's day was the same length of time as its orbit, so it always had the same face towards Jupiter. The main difference here was that Jupiter loomed large, almost twenty-four times larger in the sky than the moon seen from Earth, and much brighter, good enough to read by if all the lights in the corridor here failed.. He couldn't take his eyes off it. It was only N'tini speaking up that dragged him back to the here and now.

"How do you think they evolved, the Opa I mean?"

"I've been thinking about that. Life here probably started here the same way it did on Earth," Davide replied. "We know that life back home may have arisen in specialized environments, such as tidal pools or shallow water hot springs. All it takes is a flash of lightning at the right place at the right time and we get ever more complex polymers. Once a protective membrane is established to hold the polymers together, look out, here come the unicellular organisms. If that's what happened Homeside, I don't see why it couldn't happen here. And once it happens, life, as they say, finds a way to proliferate and spread."

"You still hold with the blind watchmaker idea?"

"Until a better theory comes along, yes. I don't need to see the hand of God in creation to appreciate it."

They'd had this conversation before so he knew where it was leading. He preempted her next question and continued.

"My belief is that the purpose of life is that it is an opportunity to create meaning by our deeds, our actions and how we manage our way through the very, very, short part of infinity we're given to operate in. And once our life is finished, our bits and pieces, our atoms, go back to forming other interesting configurations with those of other people, animals, plants and anything else that happens to be around, as we all roll along in one big, ever changing, ever dancing universe. Some of my atoms may still be around to see the heat death of Sol, maybe even the eventual, inevitable, result of entropy and the whole universe going black. That's going to be cool."

She laughed and took his hand again, leading him away from the window.

"That's what I like about you… you're a romantic fool."

When they arrived in the living quarters they had the coffee area to themselves; Mark and Rohit were in the drill dome, checking that the sub hadn't been damaged in its earlier encounter. Jodge and Anna had retired to bed and weren't due up for hours yet. Over coffee they speculated as to the nature of the Opa's photic response, how it might have evolved to fit their enclosed environment here on Europa, and what implications it might have for their ongoing research. But they both knew that the A.I. was going to have to do the hard yards on this one; the dance was too complex to be easily understood.

When they got back to the lab the A.I. spoke in that strange flat voice of hers.

"I believe we are making progress," she said.

The holovid showed that the Opas in the flask were now congregated in two groups of six, each group orbiting the other in a spiral first up, then back down the length of the tube.

"I have determined several different rhythmic structures that they will respond to," the A.I. said. It played a sequence of notes accompanied by flashes of coloured light around the flask. The Opas split into three groups of four, then four groups of three, then back to the groups of six and the spiral.

"There may well be a sequence that will cause them to disentangle completely, but that has not yet made itself evident," the A.I said. "Estimated time to resolution, five hours and fourteen minutes."

N'tini stifled a yawn with the back of her hand.

"We should get our heads down for a few hours. If I know Jodge, he'll have already persuaded Anna to let him take the sub back down. We need to be wide awake by then, and hopefully have something from the A.I. that can help him."

Davide grinned.

"You could have said that before we had coffee. I'm wide awake right now."

She took his hand again.

"Then let's see what we can do about that."

They turned away from the console so they didn't see the next stage of the A.I.'s experiment. The two groups of six pulsed in a bright rainbow aurora, their surface shimmered, their cells divided.

Two groups of twelve traversed the tube in a co-orbital vertical spiral.

The Opas danced.

CHAPTER 3

Rohit liked the quiet moments. It was one of the reasons he'd wanted to get into space in the first place. He'd been raised in New Delhi, a warren of old and new streets seemingly filled to the brim with people. As a child he'd hardly had a minute to himself, and it wasn't until he went to university that he slept in a room with nobody else in it. That first, blissful night he'd found the deep pleasure of quiet, and he'd yearned for it ever since.

He found it in the blackness of space. He would always be in awe of it, and he too spent a lot of his spare time at the viewing window looking, not out at the plain, but up, beyond the bulk of Jupiter, to the stars. That view was one of his main sources of peace. The other was being with Mark.

They'd hit it off immediately as far back as their training sessions on Earth.

Rohit's background was with the Earthside Space Administration. He'd spent most of his career in orbit in one space station after another, troubleshooting and repair fixing in the main. It had given him plenty of time alone, plenty of time at viewing windows communing with the stars. He had thought that was enough for him, until he'd been appointed to this mission. He'd taken the shuttle to Mars Station, gone aboard Europa Five…and found Mark at a viewport. They'd fallen into easy conversation; Rohit immediately recognized a kindred spirit, and was more than happy to find that they were both heading out on the same mission. They had been inseparable ever since.

Mark's background was in direct contrast to Rohit's. He came from Manitoba stock, having been raised fixing trucks on a farm under wide Canadian skies before the lure of the stars called him upward and outward. Six years on a mining run in the asteroid belt, four years fixing landing modules on Mars, now here he was halfway across the solar system, as close to the stars as any human had ever been.

Even more than when standing at a viewport, Rohit was at his happiest being just near Mark, with both of them engrossed in whatever piece of equipment required their attention. They seemed to know instinctively what the other would need, passing tools and machine parts back and forth between them, often without needing to be asked. They were currently focussed on the submersible. They'd spent an hour decontaminating the hull, and now the vessel was hooked up in its cradle, winched up so that they could inspect the whole thing both above and below.

"She's taken some damage," Mark said.

"Nothing too serious. It's mainly dings and scratches. We can smooth all that out easily enough. It's the pressure warnings I'm most worried about."

"I've just run a check," Mark replied. "Everything seems okay now. There were no breaches, no cracks in the glass. It all held together."

"Yeah," Rohit added sheepishly. "It wasn't really anywhere near failing. I'd have let Jodge know sooner if that had been the case."

"So the red alert was a false alarm?"

"No, the system did its job; it warned Jodge of the imminent danger. During our last maintenance check I changed its tolerance and set it deliberately low to ensure he would have to take action before things got past the point of no return."

"Sneaky. You were looking after his back. Just as well Jodge doesn't know that you've been messing with his baby like that."

"And I won't tell him if you don't."

They fell into a comfortable silence again, each focussed on his own task. Rohit was currently working on the robotic sampling arm. It had gotten fouled up with the goop…that's that he called it. He knew now that it was thousands, possibly millions of Opa cells, but when he'd first seen it on the sub's return, goop is what it had looked like. It was green and slimy, more like seaweed than anything, and it had clogged the servo motors in the robotic arm's wrists. Some of it was still there despite the sub having gone through three different decontamination procedures. He was currently trying to remove it with a hand laser in one hand and a thin screwdriver in the other. It was proving to be tough going.

"It seems to be stuck on," he said. "As if it has been glued in place, or somehow fused to the metal."

"Have you got a vid record running? Davide and N'tini will want to see it," Mark replied without looking up.

Rohit tapped at his safety goggles.

"Live and streaming. Although I don't know how much info he'll get out of it."

He probed into a particularly recalcitrant ball of the goop with the edge of the screwdriver and twisted. A small chip of the green stuff sprang up and hit his goggles right in front of his left eye. He absentmindedly wiped it off with his sleeve and went back to the job.

Ten minutes later he was about ready to give up.

"This stuff's not coming off," he said. "Any ideas?"

"A weak acid solution? Something that won't harm the arm but will get the job done?"

"Why didn't I think of that?"

"Because I'm the brains around here," Mark replied. "You're the muscle. And very nice muscle it is too."

Rohit gave Mark a playful cuff on the back of the head. The small fragment of green stuff on his sleeve transferred to Mark's hair, but neither of the men noticed.

Mark's idea about using weak acid did indeed prove to be a good one. The slimy goop bubbled and foamed and sloughed away. Rohit was careful to catch all the droplets in a container that would be flash-burned later, but when the two men left the dome minutes later the small green patch on Mark's hair had worked its way in deeper and could not be seen.

CHAPTER 4

J odge woke refreshed and ready for action.

His powers of persuasion had worked; Anna, reluctantly, gave him permission to make another dive.

"And it's only because if I don't you'll just give me those big sad puppy eyes until I relent. But if I say abort, you abort immediately. No arguments. You hearing me?" she'd said, and he'd agreed with his fingers crossed behind his back. Now he was more than ready to go, but she was insisting on slowing him down.

"I want to check with everybody else first. There are regs to follow, even if you've never read them. Rohit and Mark need to clear the sub for operation before you get anywhere near it. And Davide and N'tini might have more information on the Opa's behavior; they've had the A.I. working on it for hours now. Besides, you need breakfast."

"Yes, mom," Jodge said, and that earned him a cuff around the ear. But she was right, as usual; as soon as he was dressed his stomach started to rumble and his brain demanded coffee. He headed for the mess to satisfy them both.

He hurried through a plate of reconstituted eggs and lab-grown sausages, washed it down with some dark liquid that the A.I. said was coffee although Jodge never quite believed it, and was finally given the go-ahead to make a dive as he was washing up.

"Rohit left me a message that the sub's good to go," Anna said. "Davide and N'tini have indeed made some discoveries; but there's nothing I can see that might immediately help you down there. The A.I. is still working on it. There might be more for you by the time you get all the way down."

She looked him in the eye.

"Are you sure you want to do this? The main survey team is only two weeks out. They're trained for this mission a damn sight more than you have. And the ocean isn't going anywhere."

"I need to do this, Anna," Jodge said. "It's my design, my sub. It's what I was born for."

She smiled sadly.

"I know. I've known ever since we met. But I had to try." She stroked his hair gently. "Just don't get dead."

"Would you miss me?"

"I'd miss those sad puppy eyes. Now away with you, before I'm tempted to drag you back to bed."

Five minutes later he was in the sub, hatch closed, and being lowered to the top of the tube. Through his viewing window he saw Anna out in the dome.

"See you soon," he said.

"You'd better," the reply came back in his ear.

Then he was under, descending down the tube in darkness. This was the boring part, a slow drop down with nothing to see but the ice walls of the carved-out vent, so Jodge was pleased when Davide spoke in his ear.

"The A.I. has been experimenting on the Opas," the biologist said. "We think we've got a way of keeping them away from you if you get into trouble. N'tini's working with the A.I. on the code. We'll stream it to you when it's ready."

"What does it do?"

"It operates the submersible's lights in a sequence of off-on events and varying brightnesses, mimicking the way the Opa communicate with each other. We think we've isolated their flight mechanism."

"So I send out a message telling them to go away, and off they go?"

"At its most basic level, yes."

"Neat trick, if it works."

"Hopefully you won't have to use it, but we wanted to get it to you, just in case."

"Appreciate it. Any other tricks up your sleeve?"

"We're working on something, at least the A.I. is. Not sure what its outcome will be yet, but I'll keep you posted."

The console lit up a bit later just before he was about to exit the tube into the ocean below. The new code streamed down to him from the lab. He was amused to see that the code phrase to set it off was F.O., one of Davide's little jokes. Then it was time to pay attention as he descended into the photic layer of swarming Opas. The swirling blue-green aurora became shot through with yellow, almost golden, as if they were welcoming him back.

He didn't slow down to admire the dance, but continued descending, slowly and smoothly, until he came out of the Opas and into open water. He dropped five meters below the Opas and hovered, looking for any sign that the jellyfish-like creature might have hung around the area. But his sonar wasn't showing anything, just the Opas above him. His headlights, on full intensity, only showed him more open water.

"Don't you dare go any deeper," Anna said in his ear. "That's an order."

It was one he was happy to obey, for the moment. He set the sub on a similar ever-widening sweep as on the previous dive. He got a ping on the sonar when he was at the furthest extent of one of the circles, four hundred meters out from the drop zone.

Whatever it was, it was another four hundred meters away to the north…and it was big.

"This might be one of your whale analogues, Davide," he said.

"Just don't get swallowed," Davide came back straight away. "I'm not sure the A.I. has a contingency for that."

"I'm not sure I do either. But it's too big to avoid. I'm heading over to investigate," he said.

"Remember…" Anna said.

"Slow and steady," he finished for her. "Yes, mom."

He headed north at little more than a fast walking pace. The light show overhead from the dancing Opas didn't pay him any attention, which was fine by him. The thing on the sonar didn't seem to be moving either, so he continued to approach it, slowing down only when a darker mass ahead came into range of his lights.

It wasn't a whale analogue. It was similar in structure to the creature he'd encountered the last time, but this one was much larger, nearly ten meters in diameter and five meters in girth at its widest part. Its trailing tendrils stretched away below it into the depths. Every part of it gave off a faint blue-green aurora.

Jorge brought the sub to a hovering stop twenty meters from the thing.

"Just so you know," he said, "I'm not planning on taking a sample."

"Fine by us," Anna said in his ear. "But Davide has a request for you. You're not going to like it."

The Frenchman came on the line.

"I'd like to give the A.I. control of the sub," he said. "She's got a theory about the Opa's behavior we'd like to test."

"Is it going to get me killed?" Jodge said, only half joking.

"If all goes to plan, there should be no problem," Davide replied.

"That almost sounds comforting," Jodge replied. "Well, we came here to explore. Let's get to it."

"Switching to A.I. now," Anna said.

Almost immediately the sub's lights flashed and danced in a pattern too complex for Jodge to follow. The aurora around the creature shifted color from a bluish haze to an almost golden glow. The sub's light danced faster. The golden glow deepened, showing a reddish tinge and the tendrils hanging below the huge body began to writhe violently.

"Is that supposed to happen?" Jodge said, suddenly aware that he was not in control of this situation and was ten miles deep under the ice, alone with an alien beast and an A.I. who were having a conversation. It didn't do much to make him feel secure.

"The A.I. is handling it," Davide said. Jodge thought he might have detected a slight tremor in the biologist's voice, but that might have just been his own fear relaying itself back to him. "Just sit back and enjoy the show."

If it was a conversation, it was turning into a long one. The sub's lights mimicked the creature's golden glow, then turned bluish. The creature responded, the red and gold fading and turning blue-green. The hanging tendrils fell still and returned to dangling almost listlessly below the huge body. Soon the A.I. was synchronizing color changes across the spectrum, with the creature responding in time.

Jodge had just allowed himself to relax when the sub's engines kicked in and it moved closer to the creature.

"What's going on?" he asked.

Davide came back in his ear.

"All part of the show."

"Yeah? Well I'm having a hard time being a spectator here."

"The A.I. knows what she's doing. We had a dummy run with the ones in the flask in the lab and everything went as predicted."

"Wonderful…I'm sitting here alone in the cold dark hoping that a beast the size of a landing craft behaves the same way as a dozen cells in a flask."

"Actually, there's a couple of hundred cells in the flask now… but the process should be the same."

"'Should' is doing some heavy lifting there, my friend."

"Just watch," Davide said. "This should be the good part."

As the sub moved forward, the lights flashed in an intense stroboscopic burst of blue. To Jodge's amazement the creature in front of them came apart as if it had consisted of nothing but smoke. Within seconds there was nothing to be seen but dancing motes of single Opas with a faint aurora hanging in the water where the beat had been. The wispy remnants drifted gently upward to be taken into the Opas in the photic layer above. There was nothing left to show that the creature had ever existed.

"What just happened?"

"We gave the colony a fright," Davide said, "At least that's the A.I. interpretation of the response. We scared them so much that they've reverted to the safety of the photic layer."

"So what does that tell us?"

"It tells us we've found an alien ecosystem that relies on light and movement for all biological interactions," Davide said. "Where we have chemicals, hormones, touch, hearing and smell at our disposal, they are arranged rather differently."

"But the A.I. can now predict their behavior?"

"To a degree, yes. There's one more thing she wants to try, then we'll give you back control."

The sub turned to face up towards the photic layer. The lights flashed, two short sequences of multi colors. A large mass of the Opas congregated together in response, a ball of them clumping together, pinching off from the main body and sinking down towards the sub. The A.I. backed the sub off as the droplet tightened. Within seconds a basketball-sized colony was hanging in the sea, five meters below the photic layer. A dancing blue-green aurora formed and strengthened around it.

"Another neat trick," Jodge said.

"We think so up here too," Anna replied. "Is the new colony doing anything?"

"No, it's just hanging there. Want me to poke it?"

"Most definitely not. The A.I. is out of moves, for the present, but it's got a lot of data to play with now. Switching the control back to you."

"What do we do with this new colony?" Jodge asked.

"Leave it be and watch it for a bit," Davide said. "Two things could happen; it could either fall apart and rejoin the collective above as before, or it could start to diversify and grow appendages, maybe some of those long tendrils."

Jodge sat in the sub and watched for the next twenty minutes but the colony showed no sign of being anything other than an inert sphere.

"Okay, I've seen enough," Anna said in his ear. "Come on home. We've got a lot of data to process."

Jodge piloted the sub back to the tube and started up. He had one last look back; the new colony still hadn't shown any signs of movement.

CHAPTER 5

"I'd call that a success," Anna said as they watched the sub come up the tube.

Davide was barely listening. His gaze had been caught by something in the flask in the Refractive Spectrometer. The Opa in there had clumped together tightly in a small, pea-sized ball.

"Did anyone see them doing this?" he asked. N'tini and Anna both shook their heads. Everybody had been busy watching the feeds Jodge sent up from the deep.

"And it wasn't the A.I., for she was busy with the sub," Davide said. "Do you see what this means? They're clumped together in the same way as that new colony below. They never saw the light show, never got the command…but they've obeyed it anyway."

"What does that tell us?" Anna asked.

"It tells us that we're still very much in the dark when it comes to understanding the Opas. There's something else going on here that we haven't gotten to the bottom of yet."

"Maybe it's just a coincidence," N'tini said. "They could be responding to any manner of things; magnetic fields from the core below, or even from Jupiter, or even some kind of biorhythm associated with the Europa day. There are too many variables to keep track of."

"I don't believe in coincidences when it comes to Biology," Davide said.

"On this mission we can't afford to believe in any coincidences at all. Stay on it," Anna said. "You and N'tini work at it for now. The A.I. might have something for us once she's processed all the data from the dive."

"Estimated time to completion, five hours and thirty five minutes," the A.I. said.

"Gives you time to catch a nap if need be," Anna said. "Don't overdo things. We're not in a rush here. We knew this might be a long haul right from the start."

Davide merely nodded in reply. His mind was racing, trying to process everything he'd seen, all that had happened. He only looked away from the flask when N'tini took his hand again.

"Anna's right. I know it's all new and spectacularly interesting and you want to know all about it, right now. I do too. But as Anna said, it's not a race. Let the A.I. do the donkey work; it's what she's here for."

"I heard that," the A.I. said.

Davide allowed N'tini to lead him away to the coffee machine.

"Did you see the size of that thing down there?" he asked as they sipped the black brew.

N'tini nodded.

"I wonder what it was trawling for with the tendrils?"

"Maybe just nutrients in the water, or maybe something we haven't seen yet."

"Or maybe they cannibalize other Opas."

"I refuse to believe the ecosystem is that closed," Davide said. "There's more to it; I feel it in my gut."

Before they got any further into speculation the A.I. spoke up.

"There's something new happening in the flask."

On their return to the lab Davide saw that the Opa had morphed into a new configuration. It was now a tiny replica of the jellyfish-like things they'd encountered on Jorge's dives. It also appeared to have almost doubled in size.

"The cells have differentiated and multiplied with no apparent external stimulus,' the A.I. said. "I am finding it perplexing."

"You and me both," Davide muttered.

He replayed the holovid recording of the latest dive, marveling again at the complexity of behavior achieved by what was essentially a clump of unicellular flagellates. He had one eye on the holoscreen and one eye on the results shown on the meters, but saw nothing to give him a clue to solve his problem. The Opas were certainly responding to light and rhythm, but the ones in the flask here were also responding to something else, something that didn't show up on any of their sensors.

"There's something we're missing," he said.

"Isn't there always?" N'tini replied with a smile. "Maybe the A.I. will be able to tell us once she's processed the data."

The A.I. let out a loud, very donkey-like bray, and Davide couldn't help but laugh.

Davide switched off the light sources that were aimed at the flask. Previously this had always led to the cells becoming detached from each other, the single organisms floating away to do their own thing again. This time it didn't happen. They remained clumped in the jellyfish formation, and it was looking even larger now, almost the size of his hand.

"It's growing fast," N'tini said.

"We'd best cut its food supply. We don't know how these things react to an overdose of nutrients."

He switched off the feed of sugars. The colony hung in the flask, a bluish aurora clearly visible in the now dim light. Then, as if it had been prodded, the jellyfish configuration suddenly contracted to a tight ball.

"I'd call that a reaction," the A.I. said.

At the same moment a scream of pain echoed through the complex.

CHAPTER 6

They'd managed to get a few hours sleep, although Mark had tossed and turned in bed and when Rohit put a hand on his shoulder to calm him he found that his partner was clammy, and at the same time was sweating profusely.

Mark rolled away from his touch and made two attempts at getting out of bed before he got his legs steady.

"Are you okay?" Rohit asked.

"I feel like hammered shit. I think I've caught a bug," Mark said.

Getting any sort of bug was a rarity on a mission such as this, as all participants had a full course of shots and boosters at every stage of the process; and Anna, the boss, made sure the regime was strictly followed. On top of that they were supposed to be living in as sterile an environment as could be achieved. There shouldn't be any bugs around for them to catch.

Rohit was immediately concerned.

"We need to get you to the medical room, have the bio-scanner look you over."

"Don't be an old mother hen. I'll be fine. It's just a cold or something," Mark said. "Let's see how I feel after breakfast."

Rohit surreptitiously watched Mark as he dressed; it seemed to be a much slower process than usual, and Mark almost toppled over while trying to get his leg into his trousers. He managed to walk okay to the mess room though, and asked Rohit to order up eggs, ham, hash browns and coffee, so at least he still had an appetite.

Rohit left Mark sitting at a table while he went to call up breakfast. By the time he returned Mark was slumped in his chair. His skin had a gray, greasy look to it that Rohit didn't like the look of, and his eyes were bloodshot and rheumy. He wiped thin green snot from his nose with a napkin, looked at it in disgust and tossed it in the waste bin.

"That's it," Rohit said. "Get some food inside you, then we're getting you to the scanner."

Mark must have been feeling worse, for he didn't argue. He hardly ate a bite but managed to get two large cups of coffee inside him.

"I'm feeling better now," he said. He went to push up out of his chair, then screamed, the surprise jolting Rohit so much that he poured hot coffee all down his shirt. Mark's hands went to his head, agony showing in his eyes.

"Dear God, Mark, what's the matter?" Rohit asked.

Mark sat down hard in his chair. His eyes cleared, his muscles relaxed slightly. Whatever had just gripped him had just as quickly passed. But it had not gone unnoticed. The rest of the crew arrived in the mess room at a run.

"What happened?" Anna asked.

Rohit shook his head, having no answer to give her, and Mark was as yet unable to speak.

"Something in his head? I don't know," Rohit said. "He was complaining about having caught a bug."

"Help him to the scanner," Anna said. "He looks like death, warmed-over."

Mark did indeed look pale, and somehow thinner, as if weight had dropped off him during the night. Rohit's worries only increased when he tried to get Mark out of the chair and found him to be an uncooperative dead weight. Mark's eyes rolled up in their sockets.

"He's passed out," Rohit said. "I need a hand here."

Jodge got under one shoulder, Rohit under the other and they carried Mark through to the small medical facility. They laid him on the table and stood back as the scanner hovered overhead, passing the length of the man's body, twice, its soft hum the only sound in the room as the crew looked on.

"Unknown infection detected," the A.I. said a few seconds later.

"What do you mean, unknown?" Anna replied.

"Precisely that. It is not any pathogen with which I am familiar, and my database is extensive."

"How bad is it?"

"His blood stream is now five percent infected."

"Do his symptoms match anything in the database?"

"It is similar to an eradicated Earth disease known as the Ebola virus, but has many wide and varied differences."

"Can you show us the infection?"

A holovid display came on above Mark's chest. The camera zoomed in, and in again, until they were looking at a close-up inside one of the man's blood vessels. Davide gasped as the view came into focus. The cells swimming in the bloodstream were immediately recognizable.

"That's no pathogen. That's the bloody Opas. They've gotten inside him."

Rohit went to step forward to Mark, but Anna held him back.

"No. Decontamination, now, for all of us. Mark stays here, but this room is now off-limits. Anything that needs to be done for him, the A.I. will handle it."

Anna frog-marched them all out of the room. The door slid shut behind them and a red warning light flashed above it; Rohit knew that the door would now stay locked until Anna ordered otherwise. Even then he tried to hang back, straining to look, needing to see that Mark was okay. Jodge took him by the arm.

"The A.I. will see to him," Jodge said. "But Anna's right. We need to make sure it hasn't spread. Come on."

Decontamination took the best part of half an hour, what with the UV session, the chemical washes and the pills to be swallowed. All of their clothing went into the flash incinerator, along with all of their body hair and the top layer of their skin cells. They all emerged, abraded, shaved and bald, feeling red raw and uncomfortable in the new clothes that felt too rough against their skin.

"We need to go over all the holos since Jodge's first dive," Anna said when they were done, addressing the A.I. "Let's see if we can pinpoint where he got infected. There may be more of it loose in the domes. We need to find it and eradicate it if that's the case. This is Priority One."

"Already on it, boss," the A.I. replied. "But I need you in the medical area; there's something you need to see."

Rohit left the contamination room at a run.

He was first to arrive at the medical area but could not enter; the red light was still flashing above the door. He saw through the window that Mark was still lying on the table, still unconscious, although by the slow rise and fall of his chest when he breathed he might well be asleep.

"What's wrong?" he asked, almost shouting. "Tell me!"

Anna arrived at his back and put a hand on his shoulder, giving it a squeeze before addressing the A.I.

"We're here. What have you got for us?"

"This," the A.I. replied, and dimmed the lights.

A faint blue and green dancing aurora hung around Mark's body.

"We've got to get it out of him," Rohit said, "before it kills him."

The A.I. replied.

"I have him on a full spectrum of antibiotics," she said, "And the U.V.

is as high as possible without harming him unduly. His immune system is fighting it, I can see that on the scanner. We must give things time."

"When will we know?"

"In two or three hours the outcome will be clearer."

"Outcome?" Rohit said. "You mean, whether he'll live or die?"

"If you wish to put it that way, yes."

Rohit slumped against the window, slapping his left palm against the glass, willing Mark to wake up and see him. The man on the table didn't move.

The blue-green aurora danced.

It looked like it was getting stronger.

CHAPTER 7

The A.I. found it before any of the rest of them did. Anna called for a meeting in the lab; Jodge had to almost bodily drag Rohit away from the medical room door to get him to attend, but finally they were all gathered around the main holo. They watched from the camera position in the Drill Dome roof as Rohit rubbed a green speck from his goggles onto his sleeve, then later unwittingly transferred it to the back of Mark's head.

"I did it? It's my fault?" Rohit slumped, almost fell before Jodge caught him and tumbled him into a chair.

"No time for recriminations," Anna said. "Where's that jacket now?"

"Hanging up in my locker in the Drill Dome, I expect, where I left it."

Anna turned to Jodge.

"Go check it out. Find the jacket, and incinerate it."

Jodge gave her a mock salute and turned to leave.

"Wait," Rohit said, "I'll come too. This is my mess, I'll clean it up."

They left the other three still watching the holo.

As they went through the corridor between the domes Jodge was surprised to see that the other man was crying. He stopped and put a hand on Rohit's shoulder.

"Hey, the A.I.'s got it in hand. He's going to pull through."

"I wish I could believe that," Rohit said. "If he dies, and it was my fault…"

"There's no fault here. It was an accident."

"No accident. It was me. I got sloppy."

"…which is my definition of an accident," Jodge interrupted. "None of us knew that the Opa could even survive out of the water. How could we? Besides, we all knew the risks when we came, Mark included."

"Me included too," Rohit replied with a thin smile that didn't reach his eyes. "That doesn't make it any easier. What am I going to say to him?"

"Let's just get rid of the mess first and get you back to him. You can decide what you talk about when the time comes. But you'll be the first thing he wants to see when he's awake, I know that for a fact."

"I hope so." Rohit said glumly, and didn't speak again until they reached the lockers. Jodge saw Rohit reach for the handle to his locker. He put out a hand to stop him.

"Don't touch anything. Not until we know it's safe."

He went to the tool chest and retrieved a long handled wrench which he used to turn the handle. The door swung open.

A dancing blue green aurora spilled out.

Jodge used the wrench to push the door shut again.

"You getting this, Anna?" he said in the com.

"Watching you now," she said.

"What do I do? Do I get a sample?"

"No, you burn the boogers out. Right away, before it gets a chance to spread."

"I hear you loud and clear."

He turned to Rohit.

"I'll fetch a blowtorch, you stand behind me with an extinguisher," he said. "You heard the boss. We need to burn this out, and we need to do it right now."

He found what he wanted sitting on a trestle near the equipment rack.

The blowtorch was only a small handheld model used during engineering maintenance work, but it would have to do…he didn't want to waste anymore time searching for something better. He arrived back at the lockers at the same time as Rohit. The other man carried one of the small fire extinguishers.

Jodge spoke to the A.I.

"Turn off the alarm and the sprinklers unless I say otherwise," he said. "I'm going to start a fire, not cause an emergency."

"Message received and understood. I've got an eye on you," the A.I. said.

"That makes me feel much better," Jodge replied. He never knew whether the A.I. understood sarcasm or not, but he liked to test it out every so often. She didn't rise to the bait.

He turned back to Rohit.

"Watch my back. And make sure we get it all before you even think about putting the fire out. I don't want to do this twice."

"I've got personal stuff in there," Rohit said. "Recordings, some holo-discs…"

"Sorry, pal. Say good-bye to history," Jodge said.

He gingerly opened the locker door with his wrench, then flicked on the blowtorch to full flame.

The blue aurora filled the air, almost obscuring the inside of the locker. All Jodge saw was a mass of green, slimy tendrils, thrashing like snakes where the light got to them. He put his hand in as close as he dared and waved the flame over the tendrils. They went up with a whoosh, as if they'd had accelerant added to them, the sudden blast of heat forcing Jodge to step back. It was just as well he'd recently been shaved, for he would certainly have lost his eyebrows otherwise.

Rohit went to step forward with the extinguisher as flames lapped around the door of the locker. Jodge held him back. There were still tendrils thrashing around in there, although the dancing aurora was gone. He saw clothes hanging in the depths of the locker. He waited until they too were burning fiercely before he allowed Rohit to step forward.

Rohit washed the extinguisher over the flames. By the time he was done there was nothing remaining inside the locker but a wet, gloopy mass of ash. Jodge fetched a bucket, scooped it up, and consigned it to the incinerator chute.

"Job done?" Rohit said.

"Not yet," Jodge replied, and took up the wrench again.

They opened the lockers on either side, but there was no sign of any tendrils, no dancing aurora.

Anna spoke in his ear.

"Burn them anyway," she said.

"Are you sure? One of them's yours."

"There's nothing that can't be replaced."

Jodge took her at her word.

They ended up burning out all the lockers, just to be sure. Then he had the A.I. dim the lights. There was no further sign of the aurora.

"Now the job's done," Jodge said with a grim smile.

"Not quite," Rohit replied. "I just remembered something. We need to get back to the mess."

The napkin that Mark used to blow his nose sat in the bottom of the waste bucket. It was already totally covered in bubbling green slime and two thin tendrils rose up as Rohit leaned over it.

"I thought it was just snot," he said.

"I can see why," Jodge answered. He nudged Rohit aside. "Let's see how it burns."

He thrust the blowtorch towards the bottom of the basket and pulled the trigger. The Opas burned as fiercely as had the ones in the locker, and seconds later there was only ash in the bottom of the bucket.

CHAPTER 8

Davide was back watching the Opa in the flask, with one eye on the holo screen where Anna was watching proceedings in the Drill Dome. Despite the fact that he'd cut off the sugars feed, the Opa in the flask had continued to multiply, and the interior was now a seething dance of green. Their aurora spread six inches around the flask in all directions, an ever shifting dance that swirled and soared like a silk scarf in the wind.

"How can they multiply like that without food?" N'tini asked.

"Probably some kind of storage mechanism, like a fat layer in humans. We don't know enough about their cellular structure yet to make a guess."

"That's because it looks like there is no structure."

"Exactly," Davide replied. "There must be micro-organelles in there somewhere. We need more time."

"I hope we get it," N'tini said. She was speaking to him, but looking at the swirling Opas in the flask, and he saw the worry in her eyes.

Davide was watching the Opas at the same moment that Jodge set Rohit's locker aflame. They reacted as if they too had been attacked, pulling themselves tightly together into a tennis ball sized globe whose aurora turned flaming red for an instant before fading slowly back to predominately blue and green.

They're definitely communicating. But how?

The A.I. was still working on that, while also monitoring Mark, keeping an eye on Jodge and Rohit, and sweeping the whole facility for any sign of escaped Opas. It didn't leave much for Davide to do at that moment.

Anna was still watching Jodge and Rohit burn the contents of a waste bucket in the mess. It looked like that danger at least had been averted. Davide went in search of N'tini and found her, as expected, by the coffee machine in the mess. Jodge and Rohit were gingerly carrying the waste bucket away to the flash incinerator.

"This is very bad, Davide," she said.

"What, the coffee? We knew that already."

His attempt at humor fell flat.

"You know what I mean. The others, they're not biologists, they see a threat, burn it, and think that's the end of it. But we know better, don't we?"

Davide nodded.

"Once an invasive species gets a foothold it's almost impossible to eradicate it completely," he said. "I'm sure that applies just as well here as back on Earth. But Anna and the A.I. seem to have everything in hand."

"A semblance of order is different from order itself," she replied.

"Now you're getting too deep for me. What else can we do?"

"We should be preparing to evacuate," she said.

Davide laughed, then saw that she was serious.

"We've got the research team inbound in two weeks. We can't evacuate."

"We may not have that option in a couple of day's time."

"Aren't you overreacting a bit?"

"I think somebody has to. You've seen what happened to Mark."

"The A.I. says…"

"The A.I. is far from infallible," N'tini said.

"I heard that too," the A.I. said from a speaker above them, causing them both to laugh.

"You know what I mean," N'tini continued. "We're at the beginning of something here. We should be plotting a course to make sure we get to the end, not firefighting."

"What do you suggest?"

"You've already had my suggestion."

"And as I said, I don't agree with it." N'tini looked crestfallen until he continued. "But we'll take it up with Anna."

"We will?"

"Certainly. If you're worried, I should be too. And as you said, somebody's got to do it."

They never got a chance. The medical bay alarm kicked in, sounding all through the facility.

Davide, N'tini, Rohit and Jodge all arrived at the medical bay door at the same time. Rohit brusquely pushed Davide aside. The red light above the door was still flashing.

"What is it now?" Rohit shouted, but Davide didn't need to ask; he was looking over Rohit's shoulder and had a clear view of Mark. He was on his back on the bed, still breathing. Green slime filled his mouth. Some of it ran out one corner of his lips with each breath. It dribbled down his cheek and collected in the small, bubbling pool on the bed below his left ear. Before too long it would begin to drip onto the floor.

Anna arrived behind them and took in the situation.

"Can we get it out of him without killing him?" she asked, addressing the A.I.

"Uncertain," the A.I. said. "The antibiotic screening doesn't appear to be working."

"No shit, Sherlock," Jodge said.

"For pity's sake do something," Rohit wailed. "At least let me be with him."

Anna put a hand on Rohit's shoulder.

"You know we can't do that. There's protocol, and…"

"You know where you can put your protocol," Rohit said angrily. "Look at him. Just look at him."

They were all looking, and all of them knew what was probably going to have to be done. Nobody spoke of it though, they just stood there, silent now, watching the green spread slowly below Mark's head.

The A.I. dimmed the lights again. The blue-green aura danced all throughout the medical room.

Jodge broke the silence first.

"How long has he got?"

"One, maybe two hours if nothing changes," the A.I. said.

Rohit sobbed.

Anna turned to Davide and N'tini.

"You've been studying these things. Is there anything you can do?"

"I've been thinking about that," Davide said. "They seem to operate as a single organism, no matter how far apart they are. Perhaps, if we do something to the ones in the flask, we might get a response from the ones in the room here."

"What do you have in mind?"

"I don't know yet… give me an hour."

Anna turned to look at Mark. The trickle from the side of his mouth was now a regular flow. The puddle on the bed bubbled and appeared to be becoming semi-solid, almost jelly-like.

"Make it twenty minutes," she said.

CHAPTER 9

Rohit had been left alone outside the hospital room door. The biologists had gone to the lab, and Jodge and Anna went in search of coffee. When they left they were talking in low voices, deliberately so that Rohit wouldn't hear, but he could imagine the conversation.

They're going to burn him.

They all knew the protocol; it was drummed into them at every stage of the process to get them here in the first place. But it was one thing to discuss it as an intellectual exercise, and quite another to stand outside a hospital room, with your partner infected inside, and consider the thought that he might have to be flash fried in front of your eyes.

"Do something," Rohit whispered.

"All available options are in play," the A.I. said. "I am detecting that you are suffering from heightened emotional stress levels. I suggest you join the others for coffee. I will inform you if there is any change."

"I'm not going anywhere," Rohit said.

He pressed his face to the glass. The pool of goop at Mark's head was now several inches thick and still getting larger. The lights were still dim and the aurora danced everywhere on the other side of the glass. There was more green now, at Mark's nostrils, and the aurora seemed to dance in his eyes. Rohit's vision was blurred by fresh tears. He wiped them away angrily.

"Are you going to do something?" he said again.

"There is nothing more I can do. Anna will be the one to make the final decision as to what should be done next," the A.I. said.

"We'll see about that," Rohit replied, and left. There was something he needed.

∋

He returned two minutes later with the heavy wrench and the same blowtorch they'd used in burning the contents of the lockers and waste bucket.

"Open the door," he said.

"I can't do that," the A.I. said, and at the same time sounded the alarm. The clanging echoed around Rohit. He only had seconds before the others arrived. He took the wrench to the door; fortunately he knew where the weakest parts of the mechanism were situated, and the tool made short work of the electronic locking system. The door swished open, and closed again at his back as he stepped into the medical room.

The aurora danced around him.

He stepped forward to the bed, lighting the blowtorch as he went.

Anna spoke in his ear, loud even above the blare of the alarm.

"What do you think you're doing?"

"Something you should have done already," he said.

He stepped forward and carefully applied the blowtorch to the air above the jelly-like pool below Mark's ear. The result was immediate; the slimy substance retracted, pinching itself into a ball. Rohit used the wrench to swipe it off the bed and onto the floor, where he bent and applied the torch to it, closer this time, washing flames over the surface.

It burned with a bright blue glow, going up as if an accelerant had been applied to it and within seconds there was nothing of it left but ash.

He turned back to Mark. There was no sign of green at his lips or nostrils, and the aurora, while still present, was now only just visible around his body. The Opa had retreated back inside of him.

"What have you done?" Anna said in his ear.

"It's retreated," Rohit said. "I've bought him some time, given him a chance."

The A.I. spoke.

"Possibly. Although you have also concentrated the Opa in his bloodstream again, and his immune system is already struggling. If you have indeed bought him time, it is only minutes at the most."

"Minutes I'll never get again with him," Rohit said. He wanted to take Mark's hand, sit by his side and talk of better days. But he also knew that every second he spent in the room was a second closer to getting infected. He turned to the door to leave.

Jodge held it shut against him and Anna was working on the lock.

"Let me out."

"You know we can't do that," Jodge said. "You're both quarantined now, until this is over."

Rohit showed Jodge the wrench.

"You think this might have another job to do?"

Jodge smiled grimly.

"If you break your way out, the whole place is done for… the whole mission. Is that what you want? Is that what Mark would want?"

"Don't you dare try to blackmail me with his name. Don't you dare."

Rohit felt new tears in his eyes. The adrenalin burst was wearing off now and the shakes came on in its place. He dropped the wrench to the floor.

"I couldn't just let him…"

"I know," Anna said softly in the com in his ear. "Hang tight, big man. We'll get you out of there."

Rohit slumped to the floor, his back to the door, looking up at where Mark lay on the bed.

The dancing aurora looked stronger already.

CHAPTER 10

J odge made sure that Anna had fixed the door lock before standing away. At least Rohit had calmed down, but with both their engineers effectively quarantined Jodge knew the mission was now in trouble.

"Well, this is a shitshow," he said.

"You don't know the half of it," Davide said in his ear. "You'd better get through here to the lab."

"What's the problem?" Jodge asked.

The A.I. responded.

"There's been another outbreak."

Jodge turned to Anna.

"You go," she said. "I'll stay and watch here."

Jodge headed for the lab at a flat run. He arrived to find thick smoke hanging in the air and the spectrometer, and all the equipment near it, burned and blackened.

"What happened?"

"It's easiest if we show you," Davide said, and called up the holovid.

There were two holos, one showing the medical room, where Rohit was working on the door lock with the wrench, the other showing the lab area. Davide was standing near the spectrometer, N'tini was over by the main terminal. The view zoomed in on the lab holo to show the Opa flask sitting in place inside the Refractive Spectrometer. Davide's voice came through the holo.

"Any ideas?" he asked N'tini. "We need something that will give it a fright, like last time, but we also need the Opa to vacate Mark's body. I don't have a clue how to go about that part."

In the medical room Rohit got the door open and stepped inside, switching on the blowtorch. He stepped forward and applied it to the Opas.

The result in the flask in the lab was immediate, as if it too had had heat applied to it. The Opas inside didn't contract though, instead they surged and swelled. The crack of glass breaking came loud through the holo.

"Get back," N'tini shouted.

The flask exploded into myriad fragments, spraying glass and chrome and green slime all over the surface of the spectrometer and the surrounding equipment. The A.I. applied flash burn protocol immediately and all that side of the lab was soon aflame. It burned for a minute before the sprinklers overhead kicked in and doused the fire. Davide had stepped back and was now at N'tini's side, but backed away when she reached for him.

"No. Check me over; did I get any on me? I was close when it blew."

N'tini checked Davide thoroughly from head to toe, and had the A.I. dim the lights to check for aurora. She let out a sigh of relief.

"You're clean. The lab's clean."

Jodge looked away from the holo to Davide and N'tini.

"You got it all? You're sure?"

Davide nodded, and was about to speak but was interrupted by the A.I.

"I'm afraid not," the A.I. said. "I've just finished scanning the recordings of the incident. You need to see this."

The holovid came on. It showed the Refractive Spectrometer, just at the point when the flask exploded. The A.I. had the vid running in slo-mo. The camera followed one particular patch of the green material as it blew out of the spectrometer. They followed its long curved trajectory until it hit the floor. N'tini gasped as the seemingly inert blob of material immediately split into three distinct parts, each part moving away from the others with rapidity across the floor, although with no visible means of propulsion.

"It's the cilia," the A.I. said without prompting. "A great many of them moving at once have the same effect as many tiny legs."

The three pieces of the green were still moving away fast from the spectrometer as the flash-fire from above washed over the equipment, obliterating the view of the floor.

"Did we get them?" Jodge asked.

"I'm afraid not," the A.I. replied.

The point of view switched. They were now looking along the floor, at floor level, towards the lab door out into the corridor. The camera zoomed in. Two green shapes were scuttling away out of the doorway, each little more than an inch long. They were no longer amorphous blobs; they had definite heads, what looked like small tentacles erupting from them, and legs, a dozen of them, six on either side. One of them looked back at the camera from a pair of very human-looking eyes, and then they were gone.

"What the hell was that?" Jodge said.

"More analogues," N'tini replied. "They're adapting to fit a new environment."

"Can you track them?" Jodge asked.

"I am currently scanning the whole facility with every resource available," the A.I. replied. "Thus far we have detected no sign of them."

"So they could be anywhere?"

"Given their perceived aversion to bright light, I have been concentrating on the darker areas, looking for aurora. I will inform you as soon as I find them."

"Yeah, good luck with that," Jodge said, and turned to the biologists.

"If you were an Opa colony, now mobile and active, where would you go first?"

"Where any creature goes," N'tini said immediately. "In search of water, food and shelter, probably in that order."

"Right. The A.I. can check the dark areas, the shelter, I'll go check our water unit, you two check out the galley and stores. No heroics. Don't try to take them out on your own, call for help if you find them; I'll come running."

Jodge left the lab, and checked in with Anna on the com.

"Did you catch any of that?"

"Most of it. We've got to find them, and fast before…"

"I know. They're persistent, I'll give them that. How are our boys?"

"Still with us, for now," Anna said. "Do you need me?"

"No, best stay with them, make sure they're contained. We'll do the legwork."

He signed off the call and headed for the Drill Dome. Rohit had had the right idea in that department; a blowtorch was what was needed here now… but by the looks of things he needed a damned big one.

He found what he was looking for in the equipment rack, a heavy-duty blowtorch that was worn like a knapsack and operated via a one handed pistol grip. It was normally used to clean crud off submersible hulls at low settings, but Jorge knew that when turned up high it could incinerate just about anything in its path. Between that and the overhead flash-fire system he was confident that they'd be able to take care of the Opas.

If only we can find them first.

He strapped on the blowtorch unit and headed back towards the living quarters and the water tank.

CHAPTER 11

"**W**hat do we do if we find them?" N'tini asked.

They walked, hand in hand, through the small mess, making for the large larder that was built into the outer shell of the dome.

"We get the A.I. to fry them," Davide replied.

"And if they're in the food supply, and we fry all of that, what then?" N'tini asked.

"We'll have to deal with that when the time comes."

They approached the larder door.

"Dim the lights," Davide said.

The overheads went dim, throwing the door area into shadow. There was no sign of aurora.

"We're in big trouble now, you know that, right?" N'tini said.

"I knew as soon as I saw them scuttle across the floor on the holo," Davide replied. "They're adapting fast."

"We've given them a new playground," N'tini replied. "And I think they're planning to expand to fill it."

"We'll get them," Davide said, trying to hide the increasing worry and doubt that was creeping in. He gripped her hand tighter and reached for the larder door with his other hand.

The door swung open to reveal only the expected stores of dried goods sitting in their containers waiting to be reconstituted. There was no sign that anything had been tampered with. They moved some boxes around, checking beyond them and into corners, but found nothing untoward.

"Well, at least the coffee's safe," Davide said. "Although I don't know if that's a blessing or a curse. Everything's good in here."

"What about the freezer?" N'tini asked.

"Too cold."

"For us, maybe, but not for them."

"I see your point."

They stepped across to the large refrigerator. N'tini's hand gripped his tight. He felt the same tension in her that he felt in himself.

This is lunacy. We don't have a weapon.

Despite his misgivings he swung open the heavy door.

A wash of blue-green aurora hung over everything, and small green, insect-like things, at least twenty of them, ran over and around all the contents of the eight-foot cube that held their refrigerated food stores. Two of the insects. sensing an opening, immediately started to scuttle towards them. Davide slammed the door shut, squishing them against the inside frame.

He addressed the A.I.

"Can you flash-fry the inside of the freezer, but just the inside of the freezer?"

"Yes, but you will lose a great deal of your supplies."

"We'll have to cope. Do it."

They heard a distant whooshing sound. David stepped forward and put a hand on the door, and had to draw it away again; the heat was intensifying rapidly inside. Thin smoke crept through the door's seals. They heard another whoosh, water this time. He had to shield his hand with the sleeve of his shirt to pull the hot handle.

The door swung open and a wash of hot steam hissed out. There was no aurora, but their cold stores had been reduced to no more than a large soggy pile of smoldering ash.

"At least we got them," Davide said.

"I wouldn't be so sure," N'tini replied.

She pointed to the rear of the unit, high up at the air vent in the wall where it met the ceiling. It had a coating of green slime, and a faint rainbow aura still hung around it.

CHAPTER 12

Rohit sat on the floor, afraid to drag his gaze away from Mark. He heard the A.I. speak.

"Anna, Davide has requested that we flash fry the cold storage unit."

"Is it contaminated?"

"Infested might be a better word for it."

"Then do it. Do it right now."

He was still looking at Mark when the A.I. set the flash-fry action going. Mark reacted as if he was the one being torched. His body went into spasm, his legs and arms drumming on the bed, his head twisting wildly from side to side. Flecks of green spittle sprayed from his mouth and the aurora around him turned an angry red, swirling and swooping like a matador's cloak.

Rohit stood and turned to Anna.

"Help him!"

The A.I. replied. "We cannot risk any more drugs; his system is overloaded already. And the UV is at maximum safe intensity."

"Then make it unsafe. Get that crap out of him!" Rohit shouted.

Anna replied, her voice soft and measured.

"We've done all we can, big man."

"It isn't enough!"

He turned away from the door and stepped towards the bed, meaning to try to hold Mark down, at least keep him still. He stepped back with a wail of despair when an inch-long green creature slid from between Mark's lips. It sat on Mark's chin, waving small tentacles in the air, as if tasting it. Another of the things was already pushing its way over Mark's tongue.

Rohit turned to Anna.

"Now will you get me out of here?"

She shook her head, but didn't lower her gaze, looking him directly in the eye.

"You know I can't do that."

He bent and picked up the wrench. He held it in one hand and the blowtorch in the other. He switched on the torch.

"I could get out, any time I wanted," he said.

"But you won't. You'd be killing us all."

He noticed the blue-green aurora was back at full strength, swirling around him like smoke in a wind.

"Damn you," he said. "Damn you to hell," and turned back to the bed.

Half a dozen of the green things clambered down off Mark's face and another pushed from between his lips. Rohit waited until they were clear of Mark's body and down on the sheet before washing the flame over them. They burned with the same blue flame he'd seen before, sending up an acrid odor that stung at the back of his throat.

He was patting out the flames from the sheet when Mark spasmed again, sat bolt upright...and coughed a wave of the insect things all down his chest. They immediately started to scurry in all directions, too fast for Rohit to stop them.

The A.I. spoke.

"We should contain this, boss, before it goes any further."

Rohit backed away until he was brought up against the door. The things were still pouring out of Mark's mouth in a wave; there were hundreds of them, and as they came Mark's body seemed to sag in on itself, as if he was being emptied out from the inside out.

"Close your eyes, Rohit," the A.I. said.

"Why?"

"Just do it," Anna replied, "and quickly."

He did what he was told, although it didn't help much. The A.I. set the lights in the room flashing in a bewildering, high intensity, stroboscopic dance that flashed, almost painfully so, even through his eyelids.

"Is it working?"

In answer he heard a moan from the bed. By instinct he opened his eyes. He could barely make it out through the flashing lights, but Mark looked to be trying to get up, even while the green slime poured down his chest. The man looked thin, to the point of emaciation, his ribs and cheekbones so sharp they looked like they were about to burst through the skin. The aurora was retreating, now little more than a bare inch all around Mark's body. The infected man coughed again, and Rohit was dismayed to see a wash of blood mixed in with the green that came out of both his mouth and nose.

"Stop it, you're killing him," he shouted.

Neither the A.I. nor Anna took any heed of him.

"Do it," Anna said.

"No!" Rohit shouted. He would have stepped forward towards the bed again, but just then the door behind him opened and he tumbled out backwards, looking round and up into Jodge's concerned face.

"Get that damned door shut," Anna shouted.

Green slime was now coming out of Mark's ears, eyes, mouth and nose, a seemingly never-ending flood of it, and all of it with red streaks running through it.

Jodge unceremoniously shoved Rohit aside and moved to close the door.

"No!" Rohit shouted, and threw himself forward, only to be stopped by Anna putting him in an armlock.

"There's nothing you can do," she said quietly in his ear. She turned him so he was facing the window, just in time to see the fire pour down from the ceiling, a wash of white flame that engulfed Mark and the slime.

It didn't distinguish between them, consigning the whole room to a fiery hell, some of which burned blue.

Anna let it burn for what seemed like an eternity before speaking.

"That's enough," she said. "Hose it down."

The sprinkler system kicked in.

There was nothing left in the room but wet ash.

CHAPTER 13

"The good news is the water system's not contaminated," Jodge said.

They had got a pot of coffee brewing and were seated around a table in the mess. Rohit was slumped forward, head in his hands, and they were all trying their best to avoid noticing his tears.

"The bad news is the cold stores are all gone," Davide added.

"And the worst news is we all need to go through decontamination again," Anna said. "But I want to root these boogers out and be done with them before that."

She addressed the A.I.

"Any idea where, and how many, we haven't got yet?"

"They're in the air vents," the A.I. replied. "Some escaped the cold storage area that way. Unfortunately I have no sensors in the vent system."

"So they could be anywhere," Jodge said.

"And they could be multiplying," N'tini added. "We've seen how quickly they can do that."

"So we're screwed?" Jodge said.

"Not necessarily," Anna replied. "The A.I. can produce that light show if needed in all the areas we use. That should keep them away from us, for a while at least. It should give us time to track them then incinerate them."

"As I might have said before," Jodge said. "That word is doing some heavy lifting there."

"Have you told Topside about our situation?" N'tini asked.

"Not yet, and not until I have to," Anna replied. "It's still my mission, still my command. Besides, it would only scare them."

"Yeah, and we wouldn't want anyone to be scared, would we?" Davide said with a thin grin.

"So what's to be done?" Jodge asked. "The ducts are too small for us to crawl through, and we can't flash burn our own air supply."

"All we can do is hunt them down as best as we can," Anna replied.

"We could try luring them," N'tini said. "They need food and water. We could give them some, set a trap."

"Good thinking," Anna said. "But we don't do anything that might compromise our food stores; we're running low as it is."

"We could try the cold storage room," Jodge said.

"They might not go for that," Davide replied. "Having been burned out of there once, they might be loath to venture in again."

"You think they're that smart?"

"You think they're not?"

"Whether they are or not, we're not going to underestimate them," Anna said. She turned to N'tini. "You're the biologist, and it's your idea. What do you need?"

"Food, water, and a quiet, dark place to leave them…a place where the A.I. can flash burn them without causing us problems."

"I have the ideal spot," the A.I. said. "But you're not going to like it."

"Where would that be?" Anna asked.

"Rohit and Mark's room," the A.I. replied, and Rohit looked up for the first time since he'd sat down.

"No," was all he said.

"Hear me out," the A.I. went on. "It's where the infection first got started, and the Opas weren't bothered by anything or anyone while they were there. If they do have any intelligence, it may be somewhere they find comfortable."

"Besides," Anna said, "I was going to have it flashed anyway; we don't know if anything lingers in there, if anything has been contaminated."

"No," Rohit said again. "The stuff I have in there is all that's left of him."

"This isn't a request, Rohit," Anna said. "It needs to be done."

"No," Rohit said again, and before anyone could stop him he left the mess at a run.

Jodge made to follow.

"No, leave him be," Anna said softly. "He's been through enough for today. We'll get to him later. First priority is tracking down the escapees from the cold store."

She addressed the A.I.

"Anywhere else we could try?"

"You're not going to like this either," the A.I. replied. "There's always the submersible. It makes a very passable trap. We could get the Opas in there, close down the hatch, and send it back below, flash burning the inside once it's in the deep."

"And lose our means of further surveys of the ocean, with the survey team still two weeks out from Topside? Not acceptable," Anna said. "I want this done with as little impact on the ongoing mission as possible."

"That makes things trickier," Davide replied. "The mission's pretty much screwed already..."

"I say when it's screwed," Anna butted in. "There's nothing that has happened yet that we can't recover from."

"Tell that to Mark," N'tini said quietly.

Anna's eyes flashed angrily.

"That needed to be done. We all know it, and the sooner we all accept it, the better it'll be going forward."

Nobody argued with her, but Jodge saw the look on the biologists' faces.

They're worried. Maybe I should be, too.

N'tini spoke up.

"If we can't use Rohit and Mark's room, maybe we can use one of the other bedrooms. It's not as if we haven't got spares."

"Yes, we have," Anna said, thought for a few seconds then replied. "Okay, let's do it. You and Davide get the food and water. Jodge and I will meet you through there in five."

Jodge knew what was coming. Anna took him out into the corridor leading to the Drill Dome, but it wasn't to look at the view. She spoke in a low voice so they wouldn't be overheard.

"You disobeyed me," she said. "You ignored a direct order."

"I saved Rohit's life," Jodge replied. "What was I supposed to do, let him burn?"

"That's exactly what you were supposed to do. Anything else and you're endangering the rest of us. You knew the protocol. You just chose to ignore it."

"I couldn't stand there and watch him burn. I'm just not built that way," Jodge replied.

"Then maybe you shouldn't be here at all," she said.

He reached out, intending to stroke her arm. She pulled it away, and he finally realized how angry she was as her eyes flashed.

"Come on, Anna," he said.

"Come on and what? Ignore my training? Roll over and let you walk all over me again? Stow it. The puppy dog eyes no longer work. Find yourself another room," she said. "Once this is done I don't want you near me."

"You don't mean that."

"If you think so, you don't know me at all," she replied, and turned away without another word.

CHAPTER 14

Rohit had locked himself in his room, Anna was stomping around with a face like thunder, and Jodge had taken himself away somewhere out of her way, leaving Davide and N'tini to be the ones to set the trap for the Opas. They collected some chocolate from the stores.

"They're not mice," N'tini said.

"But we know they like sugar," Davide replied, "and short of pouring syrup on the floor, this is what we've got."

N'tini had a shallow lipped bowl of water in her hands. They took that and the chocolate to one of the empty bedrooms and laid it all down on the floor.

"Dim the lights, all sensors running." Davide said, and the A.I. responded immediately. The room went dark. Davide was glad to see that there was no sign of any aurora. He took N'tini's hand and they backed out the door, closing it behind them.

"Now we wait," he said. They returned to the lab. The cleaner bots had done what they could to remove the debris from the burned-out wreck of the spectrometer and the two autoclaves that had been damaged in the Opa's escape, but that side of the lab was little more than a black ruin. Fortunately the holovid had survived the carnage. Davide called up the view in the bedroom. The pan of water and the chocolate were clearly visible on the floor.

"All quiet so far," the A.I. said.

Anna arrived carrying three cups of coffee and handed them out.

"Where's Jodge?" N'tini asked.

"In the Drill Dome. He can rot there for all I care."

"Lover's tiff?" Davide said with a smile that disappeared as soon as she turned her gaze on him.

"Insubordination," she said crisply. "Let's see it doesn't spread, shall we?"

"About that," Ntini said. "Davide and I have been talking. We think we should consider evacuation and head back Topside."

"Forget it, it's not going to happen," Anna said. "We didn't come all this way to run at the first sign of trouble."

"This is a little bit more than a first sign now, don't you think?" Davide added.

Anna turned on him, eyes blazing.

"You want to run away from insects, get a suit and take a walk outside, that's the only way you're getting out of here. Otherwise, keep quiet and do your job."

Davide would have responded in kind but N'tini took his hand and squeezed it tight. Anna was too angry to reason with at this point. Davide held his peace and hoped for a more opportune moment later.

If we get to later.

They sat in silence watching the holo. There was no sign of movement, no aurora.

"Maybe they don't like chocolate," Anna said.

"Or maybe they've found something more to their liking," N'tini said. She addressed the A.I.

"Where are Jodge and Rohit?"

"Jodge is in the drill room sitting in the submersible. He's listening to some of that old music he likes. Rohit is in his room, fully clothed but seemingly asleep on top of the bed. There is no sign of infection in either location."

"And the rest of the facility?" Anna asked.

"Also, apparently, infection free. Of course, I cannot check the air ducts but…"

Anna cut it off with a wave of her hand.

"This is getting us nowhere."

She was about to rise from the table when the A.I. interrupted.

"We've got movement."

The holo zoomed in underneath one of the beds. They clearly saw the now familiar blue-green aurora come into view and strengthen. It was masking something within, a darker shadow they couldn't make out. But what was immediately apparent to Davide was that whatever it was, it was bigger than an insect. He remembered N'tini's words in the room.

"Maybe they are mice after all," he said.

Anna turned to him.

"What do you mean by that?"

In answer he merely waved towards the holo. The thing crept out from under the bed. It was about the size of a large mouse, but there all resemblance ended. There was no tail, but there were tentacles, a profusion of them at the head end, like a mass of writhing, two inch-long snakes. The body was squat and bulbous, with four legs on each side, and the skins surface was warty, like a toad's. It crept forward towards the chocolate.

"Burn it," Anna said.

"No, wait," Ntini replied. "There may be more. Give it time."

The creature reached the food and the tentacles ran over the chocolate, as if tasting it.

"It's truly remarkable," Davide said.

"It's truly ugly, that's what it is," Anna replied.

"No," N'tini said. "It's beautiful, in its own way. We're looking at a unicellular organism cooperating with others of its kind to make something entirely unique to fit a new environment. It's like a work of art."

"Let's not get carried away," Anna said. "I've given the order. Burn it."

Davide had only been partly listening. He leaned forward, peering into the shadows under the bed on the holo viewer.

"Wait. N'tini was right. There's another one."

A second creature came into view. It looked to be an exact duplicate of the first, although this one was making for the water bowl.

"Look," N'tini said. "It is made of the same cells, has taken the same form, but this one has different priorities. The amount of specialization being shown here is staggering."

"It's a fucking frog," Anna said. "Burn them. I won't ask again."

The A.I. set off the flash fire and the view was no more than a wall of flame. Anna let it burn for a long time. When the sprinklers finally came on and the view cleared the whole room was little more than a blackened ruin.

"Is that it?" Anna asked. "Did we get them all?"

The A.I. responded.

"There is no way to tell. But given their growth rate, the estimated amount of food consumed in the cold storage area and the time since then, I estimate that the biomass we've just burned matches the expected maximum range of their growth. The probability that we have eradicated the infection is estimated at eighty-seven point four percent."

"Good enough. Job done. Let's get all this shit cleaned up. We've got a mission to run."

CHAPTER 15

R ohit woke from a sleep troubled by dreams of fire. He didn't know how long he'd been out, didn't care. He felt empty and cold. All he wanted was to see Mark, just one more time, and the fact that wasn't going to happen was emptying him out further with every passing minute. In the end he couldn't stand it anymore. He rose out of bed. He was still wearing yesterday's clothes, and he hadn't shaved, but none of that mattered.

I might not get to see him again, but at last I can say a proper goodbye.

He left the room, locking the door behind him.

"Nobody goes in here except me, is that clear?" he said.

"Message received and understood," the A.I. replied. She sounded different somehow; he couldn't put his finger on it, and he didn't have any space inside him in which to spend any time on it, so he promptly forgot it and headed for the medical room.

He heard voices carry through from the lab, but the last thing he needed right now was company. When he reached the medical room he was glad there was nobody there; he might have hit them.

They had left the room as he had last seen it; burnt surfaces, wet ash and all. Everything that remained of Mark was just lying there like a discarded afterthought. He stepped up to the window, not ready yet to venture beyond the door, and put his forehead against the glass.

"I'm sorry," he whispered.

Something in the room whispered back. He heard it clearly, a shuffling, scraping sound. He looked around and saw the cause immediately. Something was moving around under the ash, a small lump that traveled to and fro amid the burned out ruin of the room. He tapped the glass. The thing broke the surface. It looked like a dark-green warty frog, save for the mass of waving tentacles at the head end. Having sensed that Rohit wasn't an immediate danger, it went back to what it had been doing.

That's when Rohit realized.

It's eating the ash. It's eating Mark.

His next moves were made entirely on instinct. The blowtorch and wrench were still on the floor where he'd left them. The wrench made light work again of the electronic lock and seconds later he was inside the room. There was more scratching and rustling from amid the ash where three separate mounds moved just below the surface.

"I see you," Rohit whispered.

He set to work.

He got the first one by the simple expedient of smashing it to a pulp with the wrench. A green-blue aurora rose around the head of the wrench. Rohit bent, switched on the blowtorch, and washed flame over the whole area until the aurora faded then was gone completely. The rustling noises intensified on the opposite side of the room and when he looked he saw two of the creatures, not hiding or attempting to flee, but coming directly for him.

"Come and get it," he said.

He took the nearest one in what was almost a golf stroke, using the weight of the head of the wrench to swing through and send the beast flying through the air to hit the wall with a wet splash of green slime. What was left of the creature slowly dripped to the floor and didn't show any signs of moving.

Rohit had taken his eye off the third one and didn't see it until it was almost on him, heading for his legs. Instinct kicked in again, and eschewing the wrench he shifted his weight and kicked it as he might have kicked a soccer ball in his youth. The thing flew across the room and made another green splash on the wall.

"Got you," he whispered, "that's for Mark."

Something clattered on the other side of the room, metal hitting the floor. He looked over to see that the covering to the air vent had just fallen off, and there was something moving inside the enclosed space. Whatever it was, it was larger than the ones he'd seen. It came forward, putting its head out into the room. He might have thought it to be a cat, if it hadn't been warty, green and with a mass of whipping tentacles at its snout instead of whiskers.

"Oh, so you want some too?" he said and raised the blowtorch while stepping forward. It retreated away from him into the dark. By the time he reached the vent the thing was gone.

He went back into the room and burned down the green splashes until the aurora was gone and there was nothing left but ash. It was only when he stood up and surveyed the room that he realized.

The A.I. didn't see them. It didn't know they were here.

He strode into the lab area ten minutes later. Anna, Davide and N'tini were all there. He was aware he must be quite a sight, his clothes stained with ash, a heavy wrench in one hand and a blowtorch in the other. He didn't give them a chance to speak.

"I've just done what you should have done hours ago," he said. "I've given Mark a proper send off. His last few molecules are somewhere in incinerator chute two if in case any of you want to go say a few words."

Anna spoke to the A.I.

"Why didn't you tell me Rohit was out of his room? I gave you specific instructions."

"She's missed more than that, I can assure you,' Rohit said.

"What do you mean?" Anna replied.

"Ask her. She's the one with the problem."

The A.I. spoke.

"I have been trying to make running repairs," she said, and this time Rohit definitely noticed it; her voice was slurred, as if she'd gotten herself drunk. "But I am afraid I am suffering from cognitive degradation. I am currently only at fifty-six percent efficiency, and falling."

Rohit quickly brought the others up to speed with what had happened in the medical room.

"There are more of these boogers?" Anna said, and he heard the despair in her voice. "And they eat ash?"

N'tini was the first of them to understand the import.

"The cold store," she said, and left the lab running.

Two minutes later they were all standing by the door of the freezer unit.

"We should call Jodge,' Davide said. 'He's got the big burner."

"No," Anna said. "I need to see right now. "Open the door."

N'tini swung the door open. Two of the frog-like creatures scurried away, running up the wall and into the air vent. The interior of the freezer unit looked like it had been wiped clean; the wet ash was all gone, leaving only smoke and fire-blackened metal.

Anna spoke to the A.I.

"I want this flash fried again, right now."

"I'm sorry," the A.I. replied. "I cannot comply."

"Do it, that's an order."

But the A.I. had fallen silent. Anna started cursing at it, but that didn't help.

The overhead lights began to flicker.

CHAPTER 16

A voice came over the com interrupting Jodge's reverie. He'd been quite happy locked away in the cocoon of the submersible, music at full volume, not having to think about anything outside this bubble, but Anna's voice destroyed that illusion with just a few words.

"We've got problems. Stay where you are, we're coming to you. I think we'll need that big torch."

He was still climbing out of the sub when the others arrived in the dome. If he didn't know it was serious from looking at the state Rohit was in, he'd have known it from the look on Anna's face.

"It's the A.I.," Anna said. "There's something wrong."

The hardware for the A.I. was in a long tall tube that ran floor to ceiling near the outer hull of the drill room. They all approached it gingerly. Anna stopped them a few steps short of it.

"Wait, we should check."

She addressed the A.I.

"Can you dim the lights?"

"That much I can do, for now," the A.I. said, and the lights went down in the dome. A green-blue aurora danced all the way up and down the tall tube.

"Open the casing," Anna said to Rohit. "We need to know how bad it is."

"I can tell you right now," Rohit replied. "We're screwed."

He stepped forward, used the long wrench to open the casing, and stood back as a panel swung open.

The interior was a massed swarm of the small insect-like things, scores of them scurrying all over the circuit boards, crystals and wiring. The wiring itself all appeared to have lost its plastic casing, and sporadic sparks of short-circuits ran the whole length of the unit.

Anna turned to Davide and N'tini.

"Is there anything we can do?"

N'tini addressed the A.I.

"Can you do your thing with the lights, cause them to discorporate?"

"I'm afraid I cannot comply," the A.I. said, the slur in its voice even more pronounced than before.

"The sub," Davide said. "We programmed the light sequence into the sub. If we get it going, dim the lights in here and switch it on, it might do the job."

Anna turned to Jodge.

"Give me that burner and get going. We'll make sure they stay confined here."

Jodge shucked off the blowtorch, handed it to Anna then headed for the sub. The extent of the infestation was clear; the whole tube encasing the A.I. hardware was surrounded by a dancing aurora of blue and green that was getting stronger and more evident by the second.

"Hurry," Anna said in his ear. "I think the light was slowing them down before we dimmed it; they're getting more frantic."

Jodge dropped himself down the sub's hatch into the bucket seat and switched on the controls. Luckily the sub was in such a position that he had a clear view over to where the others stood.

Before he had a chance to do anything the Opas showed another facet of their behavior; a dozen of the insect-like things sprouted wings, and within seconds were buzzing around the heads of the crew like wasps after sugar.

"Don't let them touch you," Anna shouted, than came through clear in Jodge's ear. "If you're going to do something make it quick."

"F.O." Jodge said.

The sub's systems kicked in, blasting out a stroboscopic blue sequence of lights that set the room flashing in bands of light and shadow. The result was immediate; the Opa came apart in a green slime. The insect-like ones fell from the air to land wetly on the floor, and the others dripped in stringy ropelets from the casing of the A.I. unit.

Jodge was willing to let the lights keep going indefinitely, but the system had other ideas. Something sparked in the control panel and there was a smell of smoke; one of the main boards had just gotten overloaded and blown. The lights cut off all at once. Jodge cut the sub's power. Repairs were going to be needed.

But not now.

He clambered out to join the others again, all standing, surveying the ruin of the A.I. unit.

"Can we clean it up and start repairs?" Anna asked.

"Not without exposing ourselves to the green goop," Rohit replied. "It's still alive, right?"

Davide nodded.

"And it could start clumping and colonizing again at any time. We need to wash it all off, decontaminate before we start."

"How do we do that?"

N'tini spoke first.

"A strong enough burst of UV might do it."

Anna addressed the A.I.

"Can you help?"

There was no reply.

"Guess not. Can we cook up a portable UV system quickly?"

Rohit nodded.

"I'll need to cannibalize some stuff from the sub. Give me half an hour."

"Jodge, you stay and help Rohit. The rest of us will be in the lab. We need to find a way to track these boogers, and we need it fast."

As the other three left Rohit addressed the A.I.

"Can you put the lights back up?"

The lights brightened, but didn't reach full strength, and they flickered every few seconds.

"Guess that'll have to do,' Rohit said. "Come on, Jodge. We've got work to do."

As it turned out, Jodge was mostly a spectator for the next twenty minutes, watching with a degree of admiration as Rohit took apart machines and built another from the parts with steady hands and nimble fingers. Jodges didn't speak, unwilling to break the other man's concentration.

I wouldn't know what to say to him anyway.

Anna spoke in his ear about fifteen minutes after they'd headed for the lab.

"We've done a sweep of the Lab Dome, as much as we can anyway. All clear so far. Headed for the living quarters now."

Judges looked away from Rohit and back at the A.I. unit. Just in time it seemed, for the green slime was on the move. The wet splats that had been the fallen insects were sliding across the floor, heading for the base of the unit where there was a bubbling pool of green where the slime had dripped to the floor. It had already coagulated into a jelly-like substance, and was in the process of clumping together into a firmer ball.

Anna had left with the large blowtorch, but the small one was by Rohit's side next to the heavy wrench. Jodge took them both and headed for the A.I. unit, switching on the blowtorch as he went. In just the few seconds it took him to cross the floor, the blob of green matter sprouted legs. Small tentacles burst from one end and tasted the air. Jodge thought it might try to escape, maybe head up and into the unit again, but the thing had other ideas. It came apart in a second, not into its component slime, but into several dozen of the insect things. Wings sprouted in the blink of an eye and in another second they were buzzing in a cloud around Jodge's head.

He tried to keep them at bay, flailing around with both the blowtorch and the wrench. One of the things landed by his ear. He yelped, more in fear than in pain, and dropped the wrench to slap his palm against it. He felt wetness in his earhole.

Rohit spoke behind him.

"Stand still and close your eyes. I've got this."

It took every bit of resolve Jodge could muster. He heard the insects buzz around him, felt a flutter of wings at the tip of his nose. Then there was a loud electric hum. His skin felt prickly around his face and neck, and the sound of buzzing insects was replaced by soft splashes on the floor at his feet.

"You're clear," Rohit said.

Jodge opened his eyes and saw Rohit bent to the floor washing what looked like a blue-light flashlight over the green slime that was splattered there. The slime went black and smoked, then turned gray and as fine as dust.

"Got you, you boogers," Rohit whispered.

Two seconds later a squeal echoed through the facility from the direction of the living quarters.

CHAPTER 17

Davide relaxed, if only a little. The A.I. might be down, but the light show in the Drill Dome had done its job and Rohit was working on getting it back. Meanwhile they'd done a full sweep of the Lab Dome and found no evidence of the Opas, and they were halfway through a sweep of the living quarters having found nothing untoward. Maybe they'd been worrying unduly.

Anna walked ahead of them, with Davide and N'tini hand in hand behind her. They were approaching the bedroom where they'd laid the trap earlier, and it was only as Anna was pushing open the door that he remembered.

They eat ash.

His heart was in his mouth as the door opened, revealing only darkness beyond.

"Can you put the lights up?" Anna said, but the A.I. still didn't respond. Anna stepped forward into the door frame. At the same instant a blue green aurora flared inside the room and something moved in the darkness. N'tini let out an instinctive shriek of surprise. A creature the size of a large dog leapt out of the darkness, knocking Anna off her feet. She tumbled backwards, overbalancing both Davide and N'tini in the motion.

We're done for, Davide thought, but the beast seemed only intent on escape. Davide had to roll aside to try to get his legs under him and only caught a glimpse of it as it went round the curve of the dome and out of sight in the corridor. It loped like a wolf although it had six legs. Like everything else they'd seen so far it was green and warty but, for the first time, Davide felt a real fear grip at him. This wasn't anything like an insect or a frog or even like the cat-thing Rohit had reported. Despite the fact that the beast had tentacles instead of fangs or teeth, this was most definitely a predator.

And we're likely to be the prey.

"Where did it go?" Anna shouted as she got to her feet.

"It was heading towards the mess last I saw of it," Ntine replied.

Jodge came over the com.

"Is everyone okay?"

"A minor scare," Anna said. "We've got bigger company."

"Do you need me?"

"No. Stay with Rohit. Get the A.I. back online if you can. We'll deal with this booger."

Anna sounded a lot more confident than Davide felt, and he was keenly aware of his lack of a weapon as they made for the mess area. Even with Anna going first Davide felt exposed, aware that an attack might come from anywhere.

"We've lost control of this situation," N'tini said. "We should be evacuating."

"I agree,' Davide added.

"Lucky for me this isn't a democracy. Head for the lander if it'll make you feel any better being in there," Anna replied. "But nobody's leaving until these things are eradicated. Am I clear?"

Hiding in the Lander certainly sounded like a better prospect than blundering about the domes with no real plan in mind, but once again Davide held his peace; he owed that much to the team at least. He felt N'tini squeeze his hand and knew that she had come to the same conclusion.

But the lander option is looking better all the time.

Anna entered the mess first. The lights were flickering constantly now, but the stroboscopic effect actually made Davide feel less exposed; it reminded him of how they'd disincorporated the Opas back in the Drill Dome. Perhaps the flickers would have a similar effect here.

It was quiet in the mess room, the only sound was the slight buzz from the flickering lights and their own footsteps on the floor.

"Can you see it?" N'tini whispered.

"You'll know as soon as I do, trust me," Anna replied. "Now quiet. We know it's here, it knows we're here, and our only advantage is this blowtorch. Just stay behind me and make sure you don't get torched."

They did a sweep of the room. There was no sign of the dog-thing.

"Where did it go?" Davide asked.

Anna moved a table aside from against the wall to reveal a low grill at floor level. It was coated in more of the green slime material and a faint aurora hung around it.

"It went through there," she said.

"That dog-thing? No, it was too big."

"Only until it was too small," Anna replied. "We've seen how quickly they can change, and how fast they can move."

She washed flame over the grille until the aurora faded and there was only ash remaining. Even then she kept burning, until the ash itself was reduced to only a black smear on the metal grille.

CHAPTER 18

Rohit watched as Jodge touched his ear gingerly. It came away with a black smudge on his fingertip.

Rohit smiled thinly.

"I may have overdone the strength of the UV. Looks like I've given you a tan."

Jodge's face looked pink and shiny, as if stretched too tightly over his cheekbones.

"Thanks, man," Jodge said. "I owe you one."

"Let's see whether the A.I. can be saved before I start calling in favors," Rohit said, and stepped up to the tube containing the A.I. hardware. He aimed his UV lamp at the open panel and washed the blue light backwards and forwards. The result was immediate; the dripping slime turned black, then gray and fell to the floor slowly in a swirling column of fine ash. Inside the unit the circuit boards continued to spark and crackle with short circuits. He saw that most of the wiring was indeed stripped of its casing and some of the boards were blackened and burned out. At least two of the crystals were shattered.

He stepped forward and chanced a look up through the open panel to the rest of the tube. There was a rustling, scraping sound up there; more of the insect things, still working away in the dark, safe from the earlier light show and from the UV. He put the lamp inside the tube and aimed it upwards.

After a minute some fine ash fell down towards him. He removed his hand quickly to avoid getting any on him. The rustling continued high up in the tube.

"Can we fix it?" Jodge asked.

"It's still infested," Rohit replied. "High up in the works, in the dark. Short of dismantling the whole thing…which is a week's work in itself… there's no way to get at them."

"And the A.I.?"

"Screwed," Rohit replied. "This unit has spoken its last."

"Could we cannibalize the one in the lander?"

"Not if we ever want to take off. We need it for navigation."

"Shit."

"Exactly."

The lights flickered overhead, threatened to go out then came back, not quite as strong as before.

Rohit was thinking.

"There might be a way to hook up the A.I. in the lander to the dome's systems though. It would mean exposing the lander."

"Anna won't go for that."

"We might not have a choice if this situation keeps going sideways."

"I hear you," Jodge replied.

Anna came over the com in Rohit's ear.

"Any luck?"

He gave her a quick rundown of the situation and heard her swear under her breath.

"Okay, stay where you are, we're coming back to you. We need a confab."

"We need a miracle," Rohit muttered under his breath.

The lights flickered as if in response.

Five minutes later they were all standing beside the submersible where it hung in its cradle. The pool that led to the tube below glistened and threw rippling shadows on the roof, and the top of the A.I. unit gave off a faint blue-green aurora to remind them that the things were still in there, probably still feeding.

"What do we do now?" Davide asked.

Rohit spoke first.

"I think I can hook up the A.I. in the lander to the systems here," he said. "But it means trailing cable from the lander bay through the facility to here. I think we've gotten enough cable on hand, but it'll expose the lander if the Opas get to them like they've got to the wiring in here."

Anna shook her head.

"The lander's our option of last resort. But we can't risk exposing it and trapping ourselves down here. I need another way to eradicate these things."

N'tini spoke up.

"The trap worked the last time."

"Up to a point," Anna replied.

"Maybe we just need a bigger trap, more bait," Rohit added. "I liked that idea about using the submersible."

"We don't even have to do that," Davide said. "All we need to do is lure them out into the open. We've got the light sequence on the sub and…"

Jodge interrupted him.

"The lights blew out the last time we used them, too much of a strain on the system, I think. We'd need to run repairs first."

"And we don't have time for that," Anna said. "Every minute we waste just gives them more eating time, more growing time. No, we go with the original idea…get them in the sub and send them down the tube."

"That only works if we're sure we get them all," Jodge said.

"At this point I'll settle for getting most of them," Anna said. She turned to Rohit. "What do you need?"

"Bait, and plenty of it," Rohit replied, his mind racing, "and I've got just the thing."

"Get set up then," Anna said. "Then we'll all head through to the lab and run the op from there."

"I don't think so. We can't be sure the systems are all operating at a hundred per cent. The boogers got into the A.I. circuitry. They could be in everything else. No, I'll stay here, and send the sub down manually if the bait is taken and the systems are down."

"That's too risky," Anna said. "I'm taking the big torch with me."

"I'll stay with him," Jorge said. "There's a couple more of those small torches around here, And Rohit has the UV lamp. If it all goes belly up we should at least be able to fend them off until you get back here to help us. Just stay on the com."

CHAPTER 19

Once the others had left to make their way to the lab, Jorge turned to Rohit.

"You're the boss on this one, man. What do you need from me?"

Rohit pointed at a large container sitting off to one side.

"The biofuel for the sub is our bait," Rohit said. "We know they'll eat plastics, and that's just a complex hydrocarbon. I'm pretty sure they'll go crazy for oil."

"Where do you want it?"

"Sitting in the bucket seat with the cap open," Rohit said. "Once we've got it in there we'll winch the sub over the top of the tube. Then we wait. The beasties get hungry, crawl into the sub, we close the hatch and send them back where they came from."

"And the sub?"

"That'll be a goner, I'm afraid. We can't afford to bring her back up."

"You know how much of my life is in that thing?"

Rohit looked at him with contempt.

"You know how much of my life was in Mark?"

Jodge decided silence was his best option. He helped manhandle the fuel canister into the sub; it was a tight fit but finally they got it dropped down into the bucket seat.

He stood to one side while Rohit winched the sub over to sit precariously on the edge of the tube.

"If they take the bait, all we have to do is get Anna to release the clamps. She can send it down from the lab. Failing that, we release the clamps manually and give it a shove," Rohit said.

"You know how much that thing weighs?"

"Okay, we give it a big shove. Don't worry. This is going to work. I promised Mark when I gave him his send-off."

"About that…" Jodge started.

Rohit stopped him.

"No need. You saved my life in the medical room by getting me out. We can discuss everything else over a drink once we're out of this mess."

"You've got a deal," Jodge said.

"Best get a blowtorch," Rohit said. "This UV unit was so quickly patched together I'm not sure how long it'll last."

Jodge fetched four of the small blowtorches from the equipment rack, put three at his feet and held the other in one hand, the heavy wrench in the other. He gave Rohit a nod.

"Ready as I'll ever be," he said.

Rohit spoke into the com.

"Everything's in position here. Ready when you are."

Anna came over the com.

"The control panel and the holo seem to be working for now so we're good to go here too. Lights are on the fritz. Better hope they hold."

The wait proved to be a long one. Jodge didn't know what to say to Rohit, and Rohit seemed to have withdrawn into himself. The lights flickered and guttered overhead, but at least the hazy aurora that hung around the top of the A.I unit didn't get any stronger. They'd left the cap open on the fuel container. Fumes wafted up out of the submersible.

"It's going to get heady in a bit," Jodge said quietly.

"Let's see if we can speed things up," Rohit replied.

He walked over to the main door of the dome and closed it. At the same time he reached over and switched off the main lights.

Their only light now came from two dim emergency lights high overhead, and the, now much brighter, blue-green aurora around the A.I. unit.

The response was almost immediate.

Even from the far side of the dome the two men heard the rustling in the A.I. casing get louder and more insistent. The aurora swirled and intensified, spreading to encase the whole tube from floor to ceiling. Green slime began to pile up beyond the open casing, filling the interior of the tube and then spilling out to fall thickly to the floor where it bubbled and coalesced, the size of a mouse, a frog, a cat until, finally, a large dog took shape out of the festering chaos.

Every fiber of Jodge's being wanted to run.

"Let's torch it," he whispered.

The dog-thing, still in the process of solidifying, turned what passed for a head towards the sound of his voice. A mass of foot long tentacles sprung wetly from what might be a snout, and waved in the air, like a sea-anemone looking for passing food.

Rohit put a finger to his lips, and Jodge got the message well enough.

There was now more green slime piling up behind the dog-thing, and more still oozing out of the panel in the A.I. unit, an almost snake-like column of it falling down into a new bubbling morass that looked already to be of equal size to the first.

How many of these things are there going to be?

The first beast's tentacles swayed away from being aligned with the two men and fixed on the submersible, as if staring at it. The tentacles wafted slowly, then faster, until they were whipping in frenzy. The beast, fully formed now, a dog as big as a wolfhound and looking equally as lean and powerful, stepped away from the A.I. unit, heading for the sub. Behind it a second dog-thing was taking form.

And still the slime poured out of the A.I. casing.

The first dog had reached the submersible. It raised its head, letting the tentacles run across the hull, tasting it. The second dog, already fully formed, had already sprouted tentacles and they too were tasting the air. Behind that Jorge saw, with a silent prayer of thanks, that the flow of slime had finally slowed, although there was already a large enough pile at the base of the A.I. unit to make another, only slightly smaller, of the dog things.

The first creature continued to taste the hull. The second was also making its way in that direction. A third was beginning to take shape in the slime, a definite head already forming.

The emergency lights high up in the dome flickered, dimmed, than brightened again. Anna spoke in his ear.

"We've got problems," she said. "The fusion generator is reporting a drop in efficiency."

"One thing at a time please," Rohit whispered.

The first dog-thing took no heed and clambered up onto the sub, its tentacles focussed on the open hatch. But the second dog's tentacles turned in their direction and tasted the air. The creature changed course, coming towards them. The lights were dim enough for Jodge to see the blue-green aurora strengthen and swirl.

The first dog-thing dropped down into the submersible. The third one was still standing by the A.I. unit.

"We can drop the sub anytime, just give the word," Anna said in his ear.

"Not yet," Jodge whispered.

The second dog-thing came at them faster.

CHAPTER 20

D avide was monitoring the inside of the submersible and had a close-up view of the first dog-thing as it dipped its tentacles into the open canister of oil and began to feed, the sucking, slurping noises coming clearly over the con. The green warty skin rippled and emitted an ever-stronger aurora that pulsed in time with the frantic slurping.

Another noise joined the slurping, a ping from the sonar, then another. Davide adjusted the view to check the screens in the sub, and let out a gasp.

"What is it?" N'tini asked.

He ignored her and got on the com to Rohit and Jodge.

"You need to get out of there, right now," he said.

Jodge's voice came back, barely a whisper.

"In case you haven't been paying attention, we've got our hands a bit full. But Rohit's UV will deal with it."

"No, you don't understand," Davide said, almost shouting. "We can't send the submersible down the tube."

"Why not?"

"Because something's coming up. And whatever it is, it's big."

He saw Rohit react straight away. The man switched on the UV torch and stepped forward, washing waves of blue light over the dog-thing which smoldered and burned, the tentacles sloughing off as black ash, the head melting back towards the body, the rear end trying to back away even while the front end boiled.

Another movement caught his eye and he turned his attention to the view in the submersible. The first dog-thing was no longer a dog; the tissue was metamorphosing, growing, adding bulk from the food it had taken in, swelling to almost fill the sub's small cockpit. The whole view danced with the blue-green aurora as the new thing clambered up out of the vessel.

On the far side of the dome Rohit was burning down the last remnant of the second dog. The third dog was also undergoing a change, thickening in the middle parts and legs.

The pool under the submersible started to glow blue-green.

"Whatever it is, it's coming up fast," Davide shouted. "Get out of there, right now."

Rohit and Jodge made for the door. Something leapt out of the submersible, too fast for Davide to make out exactly what it was, only that it was upright, almost human-like in the torso, and with a mass of meter-long tentacles swirling above its head. Rohit aimed the UV lamp at it and switched it on. The bulb burst with a blinding flash and he was left with just a lump of plastic and metal. He threw it straight at the approaching figure. What was left of the lamp hit the thing's chest and kept going, being immediately absorbed into the body.

Jodge stepped forward, wrench in one hand, blowtorch already lit in the other. The thing came forward fast. Behind it the dancing aurora around the pool was strengthening by the second.

"Get that door open," Davide shouted to Anna.

"I'm trying. The system's not responding."

Jodge took a swing with the wrench as the thing came into his range. Davide got his first good look at it. The beast stood upright and was bipedal, thick in the chest like a gorilla but with four arms, each of which was tipped, not with fingers but with whip like tentacles, a dozen on each hand and all pencil-thin. The tentacles crowning the head were thicker and much more profuse, the whole mass of them concentrated on Jorge as the wrench came down. It hit the tentacles, mashing half a dozen of them to green pulp, but six more immediately sprung up in their place, wrapping themselves around the head of the wrench and dragging it forcibly out of Jodge's hand.

The third creature, now looking the same as the new form taken by the first, was now also coming forward, albeit slowly, its arms still taking shape out of the protoplasmic matter of the Opas.

Davide saw Jodge bend and retrieve another of the blowtorches so that he had one in each hand, both alight. He showed them both to the advancing creature, but it didn't slow.

"Got it,' Anna shouted, and the door slid open at the men's backs.

Rohit went through first. Jodge backed away from the taller creature, using the blowtorch to keep grasping tentacles at bay.

"Come on," Rohit shouted.

Jodge threw one of the blowtorches against the chest of the approaching creature. It hit, stuck and started burning. It gave Jodge time to reach the door and slide through. Even as the door was closing the creature came forward again. It sloughed off the burning part, a blackened mass of Opas falling to the floor, taking the still burning blowtorch with it. The beast reached out, tentacles grabbing the edge of the door, but it was already sliding shut. The tips of three of the tentacles were caught against the doorjamb and fell to the floor as the door finally closed and locked.

Davide saw Anna and N'tini switch their view to where Jodge and Rohit stood outside the Drill Dome door, but his gaze was taken by the growing aurora in the pool under the submersible. The dancing light filled the whole dome as a globular mass of Opas emerged from the depths. Three tentacles, each as thick as a tree, reached for the submersible, wrapping around it and dragging it forcibly from its cradle to be swallowed inside the mass.

It kept coming, more tentacles rising from the body to slap on the dome floor and help to drag this new thing up out of the water. And still it came, a seemingly endless flow of shimmering Opas, gelling and solidifying as they met the air, a skin forming, warty and green and thick over the soft, slumping body that flowed across the floor. The two creatures that had faced up to the men only a minute earlier walked into the bulk of this new thing and were quickly absorbed. Long tentacles wafted, touching all parts of the dome, tasting.

Looking for food.

Davide was about to draw Anna's attention to the new creature when the vids suddenly cut out, the holo fading slowly away into nothingness.

"We've lost all visuals," Anna said. She spoke into her com. "Jodge, Rohit, can you hear me?"

There was no reply.

"Now can we please evacuate?" N'tini said.

"Not while I still breathe," Anna said.

"We've lost the Drill Dome completely," Davide said, and brought them up to date with what he'd seen before the vids had cut out.

"It's showing signs of something remarkably close to intelligence," N'tini said.

"Rubbish. It's just a blob looking for food," Anna replied. "Once we get the A.I. back online we'll have this sorted out in no time."

"Look, Anna," Davide said. "I know you're being gung-ho about this, and I know it's your mission, but the A.I. is in there with that stuff. We can't even get to it, never mind fix it."

"Rohit will have a plan. He always does."

The lights in the lab flickered and dimmed. They didn't brighten again.

David checked the console. The fusion generator was down to forty percent efficiency.

And when that goes, we start to freeze.

CHAPTER 21

There was a splash of green slime where the door met the frame. Rohit stood back while Jodge burned it down to ash. Rohit triggered his com.

"Anna, did you get all of that?"

There was no reply. The lights in the corridor flickered, dimmed, and didn't come back to full brightness.

"Comms are down. We should get back to the others," Jodge said.

"We need to get back into the dome," Rohit said. "I need to see to the fusion generator. If it goes, we're screwed."

"We can't afford to open that door," Jodge replied. "We're in enough trouble as it is."

"I've got an idea," Rohit said. "What if we turn off the heat in the dome? Everything would freeze pretty fast. Then I could go in wearing a suit…"

"Anna wouldn't go for that," Jodge said.

"Best we don't tell her then…" Rohit replied. "The panel's just along the corridor. I can have it done, started at least, before she gets here if I start now."

"As I said, this is your show, boss," Jodge said with a smile. "And that's what I'll be telling Anna if she asks."

Rohit clapped Jodge on the shoulder and headed for the dome's main control panel. It was the work of a minute to close down the heating system. Anna and the others arrived as he was closing the panel.

"What are you doing?" Anna asked.

"Putting the dome in deep freeze," Rohit replied. "It's the only way I know to get to work on the Fusion Generator."

"I didn't authorize any such thing."

"I made a judgment call. You weren't here and the comms were down."

"You should have waited."

"What, until the green stuff started oozing out into the corridor? Come on, Anna. You know I've done the right thing."

"Maybe," Anna replied grudgingly. "So what's the plan?"

"I'm going to get a suit. In ten minutes it'll be a hundred and fifty below in there; that's when I go in."

"I'll come with you," Anna replied. "And that's not negotiable."

"What about us?" Jodges said. "Should we watch from the lab?"

"Everything's down," Davide said. "Vid, comms and control systems. I think the Fission Generator is closing things down in a bid to protect itself."

Rohit nodded.

"That sounds likely. We'd best be getting to the suits," he said to Anna.

Anna addressed the others.

"Head for the lander. You'll be safe there until we're done."

"Just one thing," Jodge said.

"What's that?"

"If you're in a suit, you won't be able to use that blowtorch. Best give it to me. I'm likely to need it more than you in any case."

Rohit watched as Anna shucked off the unit and handed it to Jodge, then made his way away along the corridor. He heard Anna coming along at his back.

The future of the mission depended on what they were going to have to do in the next hour.

The suits were stored in an airlock off the lab dome, the only egress to the plain outside the facility. Both Anna and Rohit were rated for their use, the only two of the remaining crew now that Mark was gone. The empty third suit only served to remind Rohit of what had already been lost. He turned his back on it as he climbed into his suit. It had been especially fitted to fit his body, and felt snug and secure. The waldos in the joints and fingers meant he'd not be losing too much in dexterity, and the suit was rated for function down to minus 200 celsius, more than good enough for what they were intending to do.

Rohit kept his visor open.

"Testing, testing," he said into the con unit.

"Receiving loud and clear," Anna replied.

"Well, at least something's working. Are you ready to do this?"

"Yes," Anna replied. "I'll be following your lead and watching your back. Just holler if you need anything done."

The walk back through the facility felt almost surreal; the suits were meant to be worn outside the facility, and all their training had been done externally with visors down in zero-oxygen conditions. Taking a walk inside with the visor up just didn't feel right, and Rohit was almost glad when they reached the dome door and he could put the visor down. Before he did so he noticed there was a distinct chill in the air. Despite being fully insulated cold air was getting in from the dome beyond the door. He stepped over to the control panel.

"We'll have ten seconds to get inside, than the door will shut behind us. I've just ensured I can control it from my suit, so stick close to me."

"Will do," Anna replied. They both stepped over to the door.

"Ready?" Rohit said.

"When you are."

The door slid open and they walked into a frozen landscape of horror.

⬣

They had to step up onto what had been the amorphous body of the Opa colony. It had frozen to the floor more than a foot thick, tentacles thrust up like skeletal fingers at irregular intervals as if trying to escape their icy fate. The freezing process had given the warty surface a blue tinge, but there was no sign of any aurora, no indication there was any life left in the colony. Over by the drop tube Rohit saw that the pool's surface also had a layer of ice over the top, although how thick it might be was impossible to tell. There was no sign of the submersible; it had been dragged below, and was probably still sinking even now.

The surface cracked underfoot but felt solid. Rohit went over to the A.I. unit first. The interior was a mass of slime frozen hard against the circuitry. He only needed one look to confirm what he already knew; this particular A.I. was never going to speak again.

Without speaking he strode quickly to the control panel for the Fission Generator and tapped in the security code. He thought for a second it wasn't going to respond, but eventually the door swung open.

The Opas had gotten in here, too. The panel was coated in slime, the wiring, as it had been in the A.I. unit, was stripped of its coating, and at least one of the circuit boards had fused and blackened. He motioned for Anna to keep back, then removed the face of the control panel with a screwdriver.

It wasn't quite so bad inside the unit itself. Several of the insect-things had gotten into it, but only a handful and they were lying frozen in the bottom of the box.

"I think I can get this cleaned up," he said in the com. "But it's going to take time."

"We've got an hour of air each in the suits. Will that be enough?"

"It's going to have to be," Rohit said, and set to work.

CHAPTER 22

Jodge, Davide and N'tini had made a stop at the coffee machine on the way to the lander.

"It might be the last chance we get for a while," Davide said. "Five minutes, that's all I ask."

Jodge hadn't taken much persuasion. The events of the day were already taking on a dreamlike quality, as if everything had happened to someone else, and he was only too aware that he was running on fumes; he hadn't eaten since breakfast.

And a lot has happened since then.

There had been no sign of any Opa activity either in the corridor or the living quarters, and the mess was once again quiet, the only sound being a buzz from the lights as they flickered overhead.

"Is it just me, or is it getting colder?" N'tini said, and Jodge noticed the condensation on her breath.

"If Rohit doesn't get it done, this whole place will be an ice-tomb in an hour," Davide said.

"Then the lander it is," Jodge said, and downed the last of his coffee.

He rose, expecting the others to follow him, but N'tini and Davide just sat at the table, holding hands and looking into each other's eyes.

"Do you have a better idea?" Jodge asked.

"We can't take off," Davide said. "It's not safe to. What if we transport the organism Topside with us? That's a whole new level of infection."

"Who said anything about taking off?" Jodge said. "The lander's safe, and what's more, it'll be warm."

"And the organism will know that too," N'tini said softly. "You asked before if we think it's that smart. I'd say the evidence is clear. And if it's smart, it'll seek out the heat." She smiled thinly. "Trust me, I'm a biologist."

"All that's as maybe," Jodge said, "but our first priority is to ourselves right now, and that means keeping warm. Unless you've got a better plan, the lander's our only option. Or do I have to pull rank?"

Davide sighed.

"He's right," he said. "Lander first, questions later. I'm not ready for noble sacrifice just yet."

That finally got N'tini on the move, although Jodge could see she still wasn't happy at the prospect.

Jodge took the lead; he was glad of the weight of the heavy duty blowtorch kit on his back; it gave him a sense of security that might otherwise be lacking. He led them slowly out of the mess, around the exterior corridor of the living quarters and on the approach to the corridor that led to the airlock out to the lander. They were halfway round the dome when the lights flickered, dimmed… and kept dimming until they went out completely. They didn't have the benefit of a viewing window to let Jupiter's light in. They were left in total darkness.

He felt a warm hand on his shoulder.

"N'tini?"

"Behind you. I've got Davide."

"Right here," Davide added from farther back.

"Okay. Stay real close. There'll be power in the lander. We've just got to get there. Follow the outer wall. Slowly does it."

They traveled ten steps round the perimeter wall, with Jodge feeling his way with every step. He was trying to calculate how much farther he still had to go when he realized it wasn't fully dark farther along the corridor; a faint but distinctive blue-green aurora hung in the passageway ahead of them.

He brought the group to a halt and whispered, "Trouble ahead. But we've got to get past it. There should be a bedroom to your right. You two get in there and wait for me. I'll be back."

N'tini's hand left his shoulder.

Thirty seconds later N'tini spoke from out of the darkness to his right.

"We're in. Go do your thing. But don't forget about us."

Jodge waited until he heard the bedroom door slide shut then turned his attention to the aurora ahead.

It appeared to be static, and about as far away as where he'd expect to reach the airlock hatchway.

If it's gotten into the lander, we really are screwed.

Jodge inched forward. He was able to make out a shape within the aurora now; a similar, burly, almost humanoid figure to the one he'd hit with the wrench in the Drill Dome. This one wasn't paying any attention to Jodge. It had its head pressed against the airlock out to the lander, its long tentacles running over the door.

It's looking for a weak point.

Jodge raised the blowtorch, intending to burn the thing down to ash, but it was too close to the door; if he damaged the locking mechanism they might never get out.

And while it just stood there, we're not going to get out in any case.

There was only one thing for it.

"Hey, ugly?" he said.

The tentacles all swung to focus on him.

"You hungry? Want some of me?"

The tentacles waved in the air, the same tasting motion he was coming to recognize.

"Come and get me," he said.

The thing took a step away from the door.

Jodge turned and ran, trying to guide himself in the dark with the fingertips of his hand brushing the left hand wall. He only glanced back once. The thing was coming on fast behind him; arms stretched out and long tentacles writhing like a nest of hungry snakes.

His left hand fingers met empty air; he had reached the corridor that led to the Mess. He turned quickly on his heel, raising the burner in the same move. The creature kept coming forward. Jodge waited until the grasping tentacles were only inches from his nose then sent a wash of flame over them.

They burned bright blue and what was left fell, black ash, to the floor. The creature backed away, already sprouting fresh tendrils to replace those that had been lost.

"I'll take you bit by bit if I have to," Jodge said, "but I'm getting past you. Count on it."

He took a step towards it and sent out another wash of flame.

CHAPTER 23

Rohit worked as quickly as he could, aware that a single mistake here would mean losing the Fusion Generator completely. He swapped out circuit boards, patched up wiring and replaced crystals from the backup store cabinets. He still couldn't get the unit to come back up to full capacity.

"This thing's screwed nearly as badly as the A.I. unit. I might get us enough juice for four hours," he said to Anna. "And that's being optimistic."

"What's wrong with it?"

"I think the Opas must have gotten down to the core," he said. "To get access to root around down there I'd have to shut the whole facility down entirely. And it would take a couple of days, easily."

"You're saying we need to evacuate?"

"I'm saying it's your call. But you need to consider it, and soon."

Anna didn't get time to reply. The ground bucked below them as if hit by a huge hammer. The icy surface cracked and crackled, the ice itself starting to flow like thick glue.

"It's melting," Rohit said.

"How in hell can it be melting? It's a hundred and fifty below in here."

"Davide or N'tini will have to answer that; I'm guessing the Opas can generate their own heat somehow. But don't quote me, and don't spend any time thinking about it. Head for the door; we've got to get out of here."

"They can't penetrate the suits."

"No. But they can eat the plastics and the wiring in the servos. And if they do that, we're left stuck inside an immovable suit. Come on."

Rohit made for the door. It was like wading through treacle. The iced Opas were already taking on a greenish tinge, and the icy surface which had been solid seconds earlier was now slushy. Over by the A.I. unit a bulge had formed as the Opas clumped and began colonizing. Rohit tried to move faster; he wasn't sure he wanted to see what that clump might become.

A blue-green aura rose up from the floor, dancing and swirling around his helmet.

He kept pushing through the slush underfoot. It reached almost to his knees, and he was all too aware how exposed the plastics of the servomotors would be if any of the Opas got in there. He was almost running when he reached the door. Without thinking he tongued the switch to open it. He almost fell out into the corridor as the Opas left the dome in a wave. The viewing window in the corridor let enough light in from outside for him to look down at the wave of Opas that ran for yards along the corridor, with more of the slushy material emerging with every second.

Anna was still six feet away from the door. Rohit turned, intending to offer his hand. His gaze was caught by movement behind her; the Opas rose up in a wall like a great wave, six, eight, ten feet high.

"Run!" Rohit shouted.

Instead Anna instinctively looked back. The wave of Opas fell on her and knocked her to the floor. She hit it face-first, her visor breaking open. The Opas swarmed over her like ravenous insects, filling her helmet. She tried to scream, but Opas poured into her mouth. Her arms flailed as she tried to push herself upright,but the weight of the slush and Opas held her down. The Opas filled her nostrils, took her eyes, began eating her hair. Her struggles were mercifully brief. Within seconds the Opas had swarmed all over her and the suit was submerged in a sea of green.

More and more of the Opas poured out of the dome into the corridor.

The protoplasmic sludge thickened and clumped in places, and long tentacles emerged from the sea to taste the air. Three of them turned and focussed on Rohit.

Rohit fled.

CHAPTER 24

D avide and N'tini sat on a bed in the dark room; there had been some clumsy banging around for the first ten seconds until they found it, and now that they had they were reluctant to leave it. There was no sound from out in the corridor, no light seeping around or under the door frame, just pitch blackness and an ever deepening chill.

Davide swept up the duvet they'd been sitting on and wrapped it around them both, drawing Ntini close to sit shoulder to shoulder.

"Rohit will get the power back on," he said. "Any minute now."

"No," N'tini said. "The Opas are winning every battle, overcoming every challenge we set them. We're out of our depth here. We need to get to the lander and leave, before a nightmare turns into a catastrophe."

"I agree with you there," Davide replied, then paused. Something had flickered off to his right, near the door at floor level if his sense of direction hadn't failed him, a patch of the distinctive blue-green aurora. In the darkness it was hard to tell if there was a deeper shadow inside the aurora, but whatever it was, it was inching its way towards them across the floor.

"We've got company," he whispered, and helped N'tini to stand.

A second patch of aurora was now showing, two feet to the left of the first. From their size Davide thought they must be more of the mouse-sized things they'd seen earlier. They were both converging on where the two biologists stood.

"We can't stay here," N'tini whispered.

The swirling auroras moved closer.

"When I say go, we'll head for the door," Davide said.

"I can't see it."

"Nor me. But I've got a good idea where it is. Hold my hand."

They fumbled around until he had her hand in his.

The aurora was almost at their feet.

Davide threw himself across the room, dragging N'tini behind him. He had a bad moment when he couldn't find the handle, then his palm fell on the metal. He jerked the door open and they both tumbled out into the corridor. Before he could get his balance and turn to close the door the two patches of aurora were out in the corridor with them.

Davide heard a whooshing noise to his left and turned that way to see a dim yellow-red glow, in the direction of the airlock.

"Come on," he said, and dragged Ntini up to her feet.

They ran full pelt towards the glow. Twice Davide banged hard against the corridor wall in the dark, but he couldn't afford to lose momentum; the two patches of blue aurora were still scurrying along behind them.

CHAPTER 25

Jodge kept advancing, but only one small step at a time, fearful that if he pushed the beast too far back he'd be where he started, at the airlock door and unable to burn it. Thankfully the beast seemed determined to put up a fight. It kept coming for him, tentacles whipping furiously even as he hosed them down with flame. He'd already burned almost a quarter of the thing to ash, and still it kept coming.

He heard running footsteps at his back, but couldn't turn; he needed all his focus on the thing in front of him. He took another step forward, leaning into it this time and sending out a burst of flame, not just on the tentacles on the end of the arms, but onto the arms themselves. He got both of them before the thing, for the first time, showed signs of retreating. Its aurora flared, yellow gold streaks amid the blue-green. It retreated in on itself, little more now than a large ball of matter with a small crown of tentacles. It rolled away from the flame.

"Oh no you don't," Jodge said, and stepped in closer. As he aimed the blowtorch the thing sent out two tentacles, thin as whips and nearly as fast. One caught Jodge's hand where it gripped the torch, threatening to pull the weapon out of his hand. He grunted as a searing flash of pain hit him, then shoved the torch on to full blast, stepped forward, and hosed the thing down across its head.

It burst into a tall flame with a flash of heat so strong that Jodge had to step back. Still it tried to roll away, but the flames had it now, and seconds later it collapsed into a bubbling, flaming pool of goop on the floor. Jodge hosed that down too for good measure.

"Behind us!" N'tini shouted behind him. "There's more."

Jodge turned, weapon already raised. Two shadowy figures almost ran into him in the dark. There was just enough light from the burning Opas to make out Davide and N'Tini. Behind them he saw two patches of blue aurora, almost at their heels.

"Get behind me," he shouted.

The biologists complied, just in time. Jodge hosed the aurora down with flame mere inches from his feet. It was two of the mice-sized things, and they went up fast and furious.

"Is that all of them?" he asked.

Davide replied.

"Looks like it. How about yours?"

"Down and out. Let's get to that airlock before we get any more surprises."

When they turned the curve in the corridor they saw dim light ahead; the power was still on in the lander beyond the airlock and light was coming through the porthole window. Jodge reached the door first and punched in his security code.

The door didn't open.

"Try yours," he said.

Neither Davide's nor N'tini's codes worked.

They were still pondering their situation when heavy footsteps sounded along the corridor. Seconds later a light approached and soon after that Rohit appeared, still wearing a suit, his headlight almost blinding them after they'd spent so long in darkness and gloom.

"We've got incoming," Rohit said. "Lots of incoming."

"Where's Anna?" Jodge asked.

"She didn't make it."

"What do you mean she didn't make it?"

"I'll tell you, but not now," Rohit said. "Stand aside, I can get the door open."

"What do you mean she didn't make it?" Jodge said, more forcefully. If Rohit hadn't been wearing the suit he'd have tried to punch it out of him there and then.

N'tini's shout cut through everything else.

"Something's coming."

Jodge turned to look down the corridor. The first sign of trouble was the blue-green aurora that filled the far end.

"Watch my back," Rohit said. "I'll need a few seconds."

Four figures emerged in the aurora, two of the large ape-like colonies, and two of the dog-shaped ones, although these were even bigger than before, more wolf-like. Beyond them the corridor quickly filled with a wall of green, within which came scores of the frog-like things, several cats and literally thousands of flying insects. The bigger colonies came on fast.

"You didn't tell me you were bringing friends," Jodge said and with more courage than he felt stepped forward to shield the others from the approaching Opas.

"Got it," Rohit said behind Jodge's back. Light flooded into the corridor as the airlock door opened to its fullest extent. It seemed to give the oncoming Opas pause. They halted some three meters away from Jodge, and showed no sign of coming forward.

The light showed up something else to Jodge. He had a long welt across the back of his hand where the tentacle had caught it, and there was green among the red blood that seeped up in it.

"Come on," Rohit shouted.

He turned to see that the others were already inside the airlock.

He shook his head, and showed Rohit the infected hand.

"I'm not safe," he said.

"No," N'tini shouted. "We can get you into the med bay topside."

"And have me go the same way as Mark? Not to mention risking infecting everybody? No. I'm staying. I'll buy you some time…as much as I can. Go, now, before I regret it."

N'tini made to step forward to drag him inside the airlock. Davide held her back.

"Jodge is right," he said. "The risk is too high."

N'tini buried her face in Davide's shoulder as he led her to the far end of the airlock.

"Close the door," Jodge said. "Please. Do it quickly. These things could come at me at any moment."

"You're a good man, Jodge."

"And so are you. Now go."

Rohit slid the door shut. Jodge heard the click as it locked into place and watched through the small window as Rohit turned away to follow the others towards the lander.

Jodge turned back to face the Opas. Now that the door was shut again the corridor was thrown into gloom.

The Opas came forward.

CHAPTER 26

"**W**e can't leave him," N'tini said as Davide opened the airlock into the lander module.

"We don't have a choice,' Davide said.

Rohit was already out of his suit and making for the cockpit.

"You do know how to fly this thing, don't you?" Davide asked over the com.

"I've had simulator training," Rohit answered.

"And he has me to help," the lander's A.I. said. Davide listened carefully in case there was any evidence of a slur in the A.I.'s voice, but heard only the normal, slightly flat voice they knew so well.

"Get buckled in," Rohit said. "I've given the A.I. the hurry up. Take off in five minutes."

Davide and N'tini took their seats and strapped in. The A.I. spoke again.

"The camera in the airlock is functioning. Would you like to see?"

N'tini shook her head, but Davide thought he owed it to Jodge to bear witness. The A.I. threw up a holo in front of him. He couldn't see much, just the airlock door and the porthole window, but the flare of flame was clearly visible through it.

"Give them hell," he whispered.

The flame flared again.

CHAPTER 27

The Opas kept coming and Jodge went right on burning them down to ash. He was backed up tight against the door and maintaining an arc of clear space in front of him, but with every passing second the Opas pressed closer and the backpack was getting lighter as he burned through his fuel supply. He knew that Rohit would be doing everything he could to get the lander away quickly and Jodge was determined to buy him enough time.

He'd already put down two of the bipedal ape-like things, and thought it was another when the next figure approached him. He stopped burning in amazement when he saw it was completely humanoid; two legs, two arms and proper fingers, not tentacles. There was almost a face, with two small pits for eyes and a hole for a mouth. It walked forward and stood just out of Jodge's reach. It appeared to be watching him.

Jodge raised the blowtorch. The thing in front of him raised its arm, mimicking his action. Jodge tilted his head to one side. The thing followed suit.

"Another giant leap for mankind," Jodge muttered. The thing's mouth moved in time as he spoke. When Jodge moved the torch from side to side, the thing did the same, at exactly the same time.

It's reading my mind.

Jodge knew that if the A.I. were working, or the biologists were present, this might have been a breakthrough moment, communication between intelligences even. But those bridges had been burned with the first infection. Jodge's duty was to the team in the lander, not to any sense of history. He pushed the torch up to its highest setting, set the flame on and stepped forward to hose the thing down. It came to him with its arms open.

Jodge just had time to note that there were more humanoid figures emerging out of the aurora before the whole dome shook and a roar like thunder filled the air.

"Safe journey," he whispered.

The Opas rose up in a wave and fell on him.

CHAPTER 28

The A.I. showed them the view as the lander left the surface.

The complex was laid out below them. The Drill Dome had collapsed in on itself and the ice for several hundred meters around was covered in green in a wave that looked like it might keep spreading. The blue-green aurora danced over everything.

"Look," N'tini said, "by the dome."

The A.I. obliged by zooming in.

A dozen humanoid figures walked out onto the ice plain. They were tall and slender, with eyes too large for their heads.

"They've been watching us as much as we've been watching them," Davide said.

"We gave them the opportunity to explore a new environment," N'tini said. "And they've proved better at it than we were."

The humanoid figures came into sharper focus.

"Do you see it?" N'tini said.

Davide nodded. It was the first, and last thing he saw before they left Europa behind.

The Opas had chosen the configuration they would use for this next phase of their exploration.

They all looked like Jodge.

ABOUT THE AUTHOR

WILLIAM MEIKLE is a Scottish writer, now living in Canada, with over thirty novels published in the genre press and more than 300 short story credits in thirteen countries. He has books available from a variety of publishers including Dark Regions Press and Severed Press and his work has appeared in a large number of professional anthologies and magazines. He lives in Newfoundland with whales, bald eagles and icebergs for company. When he's not writing he drinks beer, plays guitar, and dreams of fortune and glory.

ABOUT THE ARTIST

CYRUS WRAITH WALKER has been a production designer for the publishing industry for over 12 years. He holds a Master's Degree from Portland State University's Master's in Book Publishing program. Since then he has provided the small press, authors, and cover artists with their book production needs including cover art and design, interior print layout, and custom eBook coding, plus photo realistic art assets and matte painted cover art. He has designed over 900 books and worked with clients such Gene Mollica Studio, Llc., in New York, Dark Regions Press, Dark Discoveries Magazine (Pre-Journalstone), Forest Avenue Press, University of Hell Press, N.W. Metalworx, multiple indie and well known authors, and currently Weird House Press.

Cyrus Lives in Portland Oregon, where he enjoys hobbies such as robotics and artificial intelligence, and gaming.

Printed in Great Britain
by Amazon

32581205R00078